Rough Translations

Winner of

THE FLANNERY O'CONNOR AWARD
FOR SHORT FICTION

Rough Translations

Stories by Molly Giles

The University of Georgia Press
Athens

© 1985 by Molly Giles
Published by the University of Georgia Press
Athens, Georgia 30602
All rights reserved

Set in Linotron 202 Baskerville

The paper in this book meets the guidelines for
permanence and durability of the Committee on
Production Guidelines for Book Longevity of the
Council on Library Resources.

Printed in the United States of America

89 88 87 86 85   5 4 3 2 1

Library of Congress Cataloging in Publication Data

Giles, Molly.
    Rough translations.

    Contents: Old souls—A jar of emeralds—Heart
and soul—[etc.]
    I. Title.
PS3557.I34465R6 1984   813'.54   84-16363
ISBN 0-8203-0744-0 (alk. paper)

To my parents

JACK AND DORIS MURPHY

Acknowledgments

The author and the publisher gratefully acknowledge the magazines in which stories in this volume first appeared.

Playgirl: "Old Souls" (under the title "Night Cries") and "How to Quit Smoking"

Redbook: "Baby Pictures" (under the title "Loving Pictures")

North American Review: "Pie Dance" and "Self-Defense"

Ascent: "Rough Translations"

Contents

Old Souls

A fortune-teller told my sister Ellen she would never live to be twenty-nine. She's twenty-eight now, and pregnant with her second child. She lives in Paris and writes that when she turns her head sharply she sees a tall dark figure standing just at the edge of her vision, a shrouded woman, moving. "Is it my Death?" she writes. "Ho ho."

I answer, No. Ho ho. I know what Death looks like; I see it every day. I'm an X-ray technician; my specialty is photographic portraits of death, and never once have I developed a print of a woman, shrouded, moving. Death, I want to tell my sister, looks like a dimple, a sunspot, a tiny dull sequin; death is nothing you'd notice. But Ellen is intense, and hates my plain little explanations, so I suggest instead it's schizophrenia, which she's always wanted, or it could be glaucoma, or it could be a loose eyelash.

Ellen doesn't write for a long time, displeased. She walked in her sleep as a child—or said she did—and the last time she came to visit me she had to breathe into a brown paper bag when I drove her across the Golden Gate Bridge. That's how I remember her—tall and bulky in our grandmother's old beaver coat, her blonde hair gone winter-brown at the roots, leaning into the picnic bag, one blue eye glaring up at me because, for the first time all day, I'd decided to observe the speed limit. Finally I get a letter. In her beautiful India ink script that is so like Aunt Carla's, on her red and blue airmail notepaper, Ellen writes: "You have always been the insensitive one in the family."

My mother was picking blackberries and put her hand in a bees' nest. It felt, she said, as brittle, as sticky, as frail as baklava. When she realized what she had done, she snatched her hand away. All the hairs on her arm stood on end, and on each end was a bee. She began to run. There were bees on her knees, cheeks, eyebrows; there were bees in her bra and one deep in each ear. It was half a mile down a public highway to home, and by the time she reached us, only one bee was left, pinned like a brooch to her throat, and then it too flew away and she stripped in the kitchen, shaking her hair from one side to the other, and Ellen and I stopped eating breakfast and stared and there was not a mark on her.

She thought this made her a bee herself. A queen, recognized and protected by the hive. When she was excited she liked to raise first one thin eyebrow and then the other so that they almost leapt off her face like antennae. It always made Ellen cry but I never cried; I wanted to see how she did it, and so I leaned forward, frowning, until she had to either laugh and push me aside or scream out in real temper, for she hated the way I stared at her.

Yet how could I help it? She was so quick, so cruel, so giggly. I wanted to catch her with a napkin and pull her arms and legs off, trap her under a jar until I learned to dissect her. I wanted to know what made a queen and what made a drone. But my mother wouldn't be caught. None of them would. And I never learned.

My grandmother started it in 1899 when God called her name. She was only seven years old; she didn't know what to do; she clapped her hands over her ears and hid under the bed. God was patient; God was firm. Edith, God said.

Eeeeedith. She had no choice. She came out trembling, wiped her hands on her apron, and whispered, as she'd read in the Bible: "Here am I." But she heard nothing more, only geese and the chickens, and her brothers quarreling in the farmhouse kitchen. Later she became a Christian Scientist, and Ellen and I went to church with her. In Sunday school I learned the same thing had happened to Mary Baker Eddy; she too had heard God call her name. Pretty soon Ellen began to hear voices, and we grew apart. She hated me because I'd call to her from behind a tree or from high on the roof, and I hated her because all I ever heard in the silence was static, and never my own name, and because the same fortune-teller who had told Ellen she'd be rich and beautiful and die young had told me I'd be a nurse and work hard and marry late in life.

My grandmother's life was dull and I often wonder what she expected, if she was disappointed. I wonder if she was jealous of Mrs. Eddy, who was not only called, but chosen. I wonder—but it does no good to wonder. I understood my grandmother no better than I've understood my mother, my sister, or my Aunt Carla. Four blonde, blue-eyed women with big shoulders, little baby girl voices, trembly underlips, and expansive gestures. They might have pulled me in off the street, I'm so different. I wish, at times, I were taller, fairer, plumper; I wish I believed in Indian spirit guides, astral travel, mind over matter . . . but I don't, I can't, and if it does no good to wonder, it does even less to wish.

"Children choose their parents," my mother says, bending over me, brushing my face with the sleeve of her caftan. "They do. There's a directory, sort of like a telephone book, up in Heaven. And children go through it and choose who they want." She pours wine into my glass without spilling a drop and moves down the table. "So you're stuck," she calls gaily. "Made your own bed."

If I were as crazy as she, I'd question this; I'd quarrel. I'd want to know how I could deliberately have chosen a family I didn't understand and that didn't know me; I'd deny a conscious tendency to pick such pain, such frustration, such fury, such—for, of course, it's there, too—such love. But I'm not as crazy as she; I never argue any more, and when I sip my wine I spill some and she shakes her head and clucks her tongue and I vow not to come here for dinner every Thursday night; I'm an adult now, I have a life of my own. I can go home and wait for Dr. Danvers to phone.

Dr. Danvers leads me down the hall to the window, his fingers lightly pinching the cloth of my smock. "I want," he repeats, "to run away with you." Since he is married, this is an unlikely proposition, but I can tell by the grip of his clean sincere fingers that I am meant to believe it, meant to have my heart broken. I look up and his hot blue eyes are looking beyond me, over my head at the eucalyptus beyond the window, to the cool white sky where we will fly like sea birds to some bright island. But he is just like my mother, I think, like Carla and Ellen. He believes in transformation by touch, in falling in love. He believes in broken hearts. I have to close my eyes. When I open them, he is gone. Good, I think. Run away yourself. See how you like it. He has kissed my cheek and the spot is damp as a cloud.

This is a family story. Aunt Carla was alone in her house on a hot spring night. She had hemorrhaged for the first time that night, and wept to see her bright red blood go down the toilet. Later she took some sleeping pills and went to bed. The telephone rang around midnight and when

Carla picked it up, my grandmother, sounding bright and cheery, said she loved her and was looking forward to seeing her soon.

Carla could not remember. She shook her head, and muttered thickly, "How soon?"

"In June," my grandmother said, sounding, Carla thought, a little hurt. Then she hung up. That wasn't unlike her, for she was absentminded, and she often sent postcards with nothing on them, and she had to keep train tickets pinned to her slip. Nor was it unusual that she'd call late at night; she always called late. When she was alive. That was the only unusual thing about it. For my grandmother had been dead for two years when Carla received the telephone call, and Carla herself—I should let Ellen tell this, she tells it better than I—Carla died on the operating table in June, in great pain, her face black with blood and contorted.

Mother left at once for Spain. "I feel as sad," she wrote from Majorca, "as Juliet of the Spirits."

For Christmas last year Ellen sent Mother a Ouija board wrapped in silver paper and Mother played with it like a child for a few minutes, fingering the heart-shaped message indicator and peering through its plastic eye to examine the murky illustrations on the board. Then, without a word, she went to her room and came out carrying some of Carla's things I hadn't seen in years: a china ballerina with a stiff net skirt, a blue scarf with roses, a Balinese bracelet. She put these on the table next to Carla's angel chimes, which she unpacked every Christmas, lit all the candles, and turned off the lights.

"Oh for God's sake," I said.

"That's right," Mother said. "For God's sake and ours as well. Now sit still. Can you? This goes on our knees. Concentrate." She closed her eyes. Gold eye shadow gleamed in the moist webbed lines of her lids and shadows sagged at her neck. She's old, I thought, and I wanted to lean over and laugh, close to her ear. "Caaarla," my mother called. I listened to the little angels go tink-tink-tink, and I thought about Dr. Danvers, who was home with his wife and his many children thinking of me, or the girl he liked to think of as me, the lost girl, the dream girl, unreal. He was glad I had somewhere to go for Christmas; I should never, he said, be alone.

"Carla," my mother repeated.

I told him I had always been alone.

My mother opened her eyes, round blue candlelit eyes, like Ellen's eyes, and Carla's. "Nothing's happening," she said. "I can't play with you."

"Carla never liked me."

"You made fun of her," my mother said. She folded the board and, tenderly, smoothed it on her lap. "You know you did."

Aunt Carla was an alcoholic. No one seemed to notice. She didn't have an inner ear problem, as my grandmother claimed, that caused her to suddenly slip to the floor along the wall; nor, when she put her face in her food and fell asleep, was it, as my mother serenely insisted, caused by a hard day at the gallery. I tried to talk about Carla's drinking, but I felt foolish; I felt as if I were lying. "You ought to help her," I said, but my mother shook her head as if there were bees in her brain and drifted off to the piano to play Chopin by an open window; she would never play, she said, as well as Carla.

And when Carla died, she and Ellen agreed the doctors had murdered her, that some people were just too good to live. But Carla died because she had cirrhosis, and she had cirrhosis because she drank, and she drank because no one tried to stop her. It was not murder, it was suicide, a suicide pact. They were all in on it.

Dr. Danvers says he met me in another life and recognized me at once in the hospital corridors the first day he saw me. It was in Persia, or Atlantis; I was as young then as I am now, as dark, as serious, as swift. A dancer? He laughs and kisses my instep. He is a tender man, Dr. Danvers, and he tries not to hurt me. He says he met me before and soon, when this is over and he goes back to his wife, he will tell me that somewhere, sometime, we'll meet again. But we won't. I'm not psychic. You don't have to be psychic to know these things. We will not meet on Mars. There was no Atlantis.

"You are too hard," he says, his face in my hair. "Too hard on us all."

Am I going to die?

That's what the patients ask me. They sit on folding chairs in the hospital basement and I briskly whisk them in and out of the dark green curtains. Am I going to die? Am I going to die? Old men and old women, mothers holding their children, a frightened steelworker, a couple of teenagers, a Japanese tourist who fell sick in Seattle.

Stand here. Take a deep breath. Now out. Good.

Of course you're going to die. Is that being too hard? We're all going to die.

"I'm not," my mother announces. "Your grandmother didn't, your aunt didn't, Jesus Christ didn't, and I won't."

No. How can she? I don't know her yet. I love her and I hate her and I fear her and I pity her and I want her to die but I don't know her yet. I stroke her hand, a small white hand with a large dirty bruise; she struck it on the fireplace when she fell. I put my cheek against the bruise. I had no premonition this would happen, never dreamed I would have to come to her today by elevator in my hospital smock. No bird flew through my window, no telephone rang at midnight, no woman mourned at the edge of my eye.

My mother grins. "Now you," she says.

"Yes?"

"You have a long way to go. But I," her hand goes to her hair, twists a curl, straightens it, "I have done it all already. I'm a very old, old soul," she says in her tiny baby voice, pleased.

She keeps her eyes open while I kiss her good-bye and that night, sometime after three in the morning, she is dead.

Ellen couldn't come to the funeral, and on the same day I sent the packet of wedding rings, recipes, and the bumblebee pin with the diamond chips, she gave birth to a daughter, eight pounds, nine ounces. "I've named the baby Bleu," she writes, "for all of us."

I crumple the note in my hand. My eyes are brown, not blue. Does she include me in the "us" because I'm feeling blue? Is Dr. Danvers perhaps part of the "us"? Dr. Danvers who fixes his hot blue eyes to my lips when he passes, letting me know how he suffers? How does he suffer? What does she mean?

Lives begin, end. Loves, too. I'm alone now—but then I've always been alone. At night I wash my hair and water my plants and paint my nails and wind my clock. And I listen for the voices. They come late at night, just before sleep. They were indecipherable at first, just a blur of women's voices, and then, slowly, reluctantly, I recognized the chunky girlish cadences of my family. Once I heard my grandmother complain about the roses, and once Aunt

Clara cried out with pleasure. My mother sings. Little songs I've never heard before, with words I can't remember. I've been meaning to write to Ellen, to brag, to tell her: See! You're not the only one; I'm psychic too. I belong just as much as you do.

But last night the voices were frightened, high and sharp and skittish. Who's there? they cried. Is someone there? Who's listening? they cried. Who's listening to us?

And I was too angry to fall asleep and stayed awake all night, but they never said another word, and if I know them, they never will.

A Jar of Emeralds

O'Connor was my husband. Not my first husband. My first husband was a boy who loved cars. I don't remember his face. I remember his tennis shoes sticking out from under his black Ford parked in the driveway. I had to kneel to kiss him. His eyes were white in the darkness and he kept them wide open; we didn't kiss much. We didn't know each other long before we got married, and we didn't stay married long enough to know each other later. We were polite and unkind. One night he said, "Would you care to look at the moon?" I did and he locked me outside. I called and joked and pleaded and would have kicked the door down except I was barefoot. I could hear him breathing on the other side, light and quick, as if he was scared. I was scared too; I stood there in my nightgown, wondering what to do. I looked at the door, I looked at the moon, and then I walked away. I met O'Connor later, when I was working for the trucking company. O'Connor was going to "save" me.

Not that there was much to save. I was still scared. I still stood on the outside. I looked at myself in mirrors and didn't like what I saw. I saw a zero. Miss No One. My face felt numb and bare as an egg, so I painted in eyebrows, glued on false lashes, rouged in two cheeks, and drew a wide smile with lipstick. No one would know me now, I decided. The make-up worked as disguise and protection; it

helped me lie about my age, lie about my typing skills, lie
about my divorce. It also helped me steal. I took earrings
from Woolworth's, lamb chops from Safeway, pin money
from the petty cash drawer at work. O'Connor said I was
trying to punish men in general and the world in pacific. I
said, What general? What pacific? O'Connor said, Never
mind, the point is you want to get pegged.

And maybe I did. But not by him. I had pegged
O'Connor the moment I saw him. He was tall and bald
and old—almost thirty—with a gap between his large front
teeth. He wore thick glasses and cowboy boots. He spoke
faster than I could hear, and he used words incorrectly;
once I heard him say one of the other drivers "couldn't
pass mustard." He gave me a headache. I felt people who
knew nothing should at least know their place. O'Connor
didn't know his place or respect anyone else's. He imitated
everyone he met. It wasn't malicious. It was his concept
of manners. If he met a southerner, he spoke in a honeyed
slur that was most peculiar. If he spoke to a child he spoke
baby talk. When he spoke to me he lowered his eyes and
held his breath and cheeped; I thought he was crazy at first
and then I realized that was how I sounded—cheep
cheep—and then I hated him.

"What are you doing with all that money?" he cheeped.

I hated him too much to answer. He knelt at my feet and
unzipped my boot. Two dollars and fifty-seven cents fell
out. He rocked back on his heels the way Cal, the mechanic,
did, and he jammed his glasses back on his nose the way
Mr. Deever, the union steward, did, and he cocked his head
the way Pete Brown, the dispatcher, did, and he looked up
at me while I looked down at him, and then he zipped my
boot back up and put the money back in the cash drawer
and asked me out.

During most of that first night I stared out the car window like a hostage. I thought of writing HELP on the

glass; I thought of waving a Kleenex to cops. But I was too alarmed by O'Connor to move. O'Connor was drunk. He drove like a maniac and he gave a jagged, incoherent lecture on What Girls with Abilities Shouldn't Do as he screeched around corners or came to full stops before green lights. I didn't know what he meant by "abilities." When I asked him, he growled something about my handwriting; he liked the way I made out the payroll, with all the numbers round and clear and all the names spelled correctly. He said my handwriting showed intelligence, ambition, and courage. I was impressed. O'Connor had made me up. No one had taken the trouble to make me up for a long time. I was still feeling grateful when he suddenly turned into a warehouse yard, pulled the brake, and lurched toward me; I screamed and started to claw him, but he caught my wrists in one hand and delicately, for someone so drunk, pulled off first one false eyelash and then the other. "Now," he said, "I can see you."

I didn't see him until much later. I kept going out with him because I thought I had to, and because it pleased me to please someone else so much. He treated me like a queen, and I liked that. I liked making fun of his cowboy shirts and I liked correcting his vocabulary. He talked all the time and what he said made no sense; I liked that too; I thought that was funny. Once he told me he composited songs; once he told me he was a tune mongrel. He was so old and odd I thought he might be a genius.

We went dancing one night—I went dancing, he sat and drank and watched me—and later he drove me to a place I'd never been before, up high in the hills behind the university. He started to kiss me, then gave up and passed out on the steering wheel. I felt happy. I slipped out of the car and danced around the oak trees in the moonlight, singing to the car radio. I felt I was putting on a show of some sort, a star performance staged exclusively for the trees and

shadows and the university lights twinkling below; I felt
the whole world was waiting to see what I could do. I was
only nineteen. I had one marriage behind me, thousands
to go. But when I slid back into the car and laughed down
at O'Connor asleep on the wheel, something happened. I
could see him, really see him, and he was the first man I'd
seen in a long, long time. He wasn't a zero and he wasn't a
genius. He wasn't very odd, and he wasn't very old. He was
just a nice, slow-moving man with a lonely sag to his lower
lip and a faint, sour smell to his skin, like grass. He looked
like he needed someone to love him. I touched his face with
my finger and thought: all right, okay, I'll try. Then I took
his glasses off and folded them in my purse and fell asleep
on his hip.

We were married two months later and I think . . . I
think we were happy. I felt I knew him, knew the delicate
nervous silence behind all his noise. I didn't have to listen
to him to know he was good; the way he held a coffee cup or
pared an apple told me he was. His touch was soft as an
airbrush; if he drew his hand across my face I'd feel my
features blur, become beautiful. He was kind to the cat and
kind to the plants, but he was kindest at night, when no one
could see his face. If I came into the room and turned on
the light he'd leap from the window where he'd been sitting
and suddenly start imitating W. C. Fields with a whoop and
a froggy cackle that startled me. Then he'd go into his
whole routine: movie stars and politicians and cartoon
characters I'd never heard of. Guess! he'd cry. I can't! I'd
cry back. I'd put my hands over my ears. "Will you be
real?" I'd say. Even when I was laughing I was angry.
"Is it so terrible to just be yourself?"

He'd hit himself on the forehead and stagger around like
Donald Duck. I am myself, quack-quack. You're not yourself, cheep-cheep. So what's a self, so what's an I, so what is
real, so who are you . . .

"Life," O'Connor told me, "is nothing but a dumb joke in the first place. It's a trap shoot."

A trap shoot? Crap shoot? Craps shoot? I'd reach for the dictionary. I could never find what I wanted in the dictionary; I could never prove O'Connor was wrong. Was our life a dumb joke? I didn't think so. I thought it was fine. O'Connor had quit the trucking company and found a better job driving for a dairy. He left every morning at four and came back every afternoon at two. I stayed home. I made cookies and sewed curtains and gave myself facials. I felt "saved" and grateful. And then I grew restless. Being locked inside, I decided, was as bad as being locked outside. O'Connor didn't want me to work but he did want me to go to school. He said I was bright as a zipper. I reached for the dictionary, muttering, "Button, you mean bright as a button," and then I enrolled in junior college. At night we watched TV, or played poker, or got drunk on jug wine and sat late at the kitchen table and argued. O'Connor was exhausting to argue with; his logic shot off in thirty directions and when you tried to pin him down he'd wiggle free. "I never said that," O'Connor scowled. I'd pound the table and demand a tape recorder. I wanted a tape recorder for proof. He said there was such a thing as a "suicidal complexion" and that all people who killed themselves had a certain pigment in their skin that made them do it. He said vitamin C gave people colds. He said women drivers had statistically proven higher accident rates than men and he said the moon had been hollowed out by the United States Army and made into a weapons base and secret sports arena. "I never said they were going to hold the Olympics there," O'Connor would deny, pounding the table back at me. For my twenty-first birthday he bought me a tape recorder, and when I played it back to him, triumphant, I heard my own voice: cheep cheep, and his voice, cheep cheep, and I snapped it off. We began to stop arguing. We began to stop talking, because when we talked we argued. We still said, "I love you," but we said it fast, in passing, usually from doorways. Every Friday we went out for Japanese food, every Sunday we went to the beach, and every Wednesday night we went to the high school gym. O'Connor played basketball with a group of other men, and I sat high on the bleachers with the other wives, my textbooks open in my lap as I listened to them cheer our team and boo the opposition. Occasionally I looked down and watched O'Connor. He looked like a different man, ashen and intent, his long arms flashing above his bald head. He was a fast forward, confused and very joyous. He rarely made a basket but that didn't seem to matter; he always had the ball, and his entire face was pocked with little smiles. I remember thinking: that must be how his face looks when he makes love to me. That night I wanted to make love with the lights on but he wouldn't let me. "I don't look at you," he pointed out. And that, I realized, was true. I began to feel scared again. I began to feel like a zero again. The no one in him had seen the no one in me, and married it. I resented that. It became harder to see the someone in him. Expressions, voices, ideas—all flitted over him like light over water. I could tell who he'd had lunch with by the way he held his cigarette; if it hung off his lower lip he'd been drinking with Roger, if he held it high and waved it around he'd been out with Mr. Cleary. The worst was when he played the guitar. I'd lie on the floor with my homework and he'd sit at the front window, his long foot on his little footrest, compositing. He composited song after song. They were all songs I knew. They were songs everyone knew but O'Connor. Listen to this one, he'd say, and then he'd play "Stormy Weather." You write the words, he told me, you're good with words. They've got words, I'd sigh. All your songs have words already. "You don't understand," O'Connor said. And I didn't. I didn't understand and there was no one I could ask. O'Connor's parents and sister had been killed in a car crash when he was ten; after that he had lived in an orphanage. An orphanage is no place for children, O'Connor told me once; you grow up in pieces there. You grow up guarded. O'Connor was thirty years old and he was still afraid to laugh out loud; he covered his mouth when he laughed, or turned his head away. One night he showed me what he'd learned in the orphanage; he took a dinner fork and bent it to fit around his knuckles. "You could rip someone's heart out with this," he said. For a minute I thought he meant mine, and then he aimed a hook shot and threw the fork in the garbage. "Did you make that up?" I asked. "Did you invent that way of fighting?"

"Oh you know better," he said. "You're the college girl. You know I'm the original unoriginal kid."

I thought the original unoriginal kid was good, but I didn't tell him. Maybe I should have. By then, though, we were at war. By then we both wished we had forks to fight with. We slept with our fists clenched, far apart on the bed. I had stopped asking him to be real, and he had stopped asking me to write lyrics. He began to write his own. I found one fallen to the floor by the window when I moved. "My libido's incognito." I smoothed it out, stared at it. I couldn't believe O'Connor had written it. I wanted to reach up and hug his knees. I wanted to tell him I'd been wrong the whole time; he was a genius, a rare bird, a wonder man. But he's not here any more. He's gone. No one knows where. State police found his dairy truck abandoned on the highway a hundred miles from here. O'Connor just parked it and got down and walked away. There was no sign of foul play; there was no message for me. I try to imagine O'Connor, with his guitar, walking over the fields with the sun coming up. It's hard for me to see him. But then it was always hard.

One night O'Connor caught me staring and stopped playing his guitar. "Now what?" he said, wary.

I put my book flat on the table and stood up. I said I wanted something more.

"You want a house," he said. He began to play the guitar again, his long foot tapping. "You want a house and a car and a kid. You want to marry a college professor. I know your type."

My type? Maybe that was it, part of the problem. Maybe he had stopped making me up, or had started to make me up wrong. Maybe he saw me as Miss No One, the zero. But I only felt like a zero at home. At school I felt fine. I was making good grades and my teachers were treating me like a Girl with Abilities. You can do what you want, my teachers were saying. You've got what it takes.

"It's you," I decided. "You make me feel there's nothing inside me."

"There *is* nothing inside you," he said. "You're like everyone else. You're nothing. You're no one."

Later, though, he said he thought there was something inside me. Later, when I graduated from junior college and enrolled in the university, he said he thought there was evil in me. I believed him. I could feel it. I went to a psychiatrist. The psychiatrist said there was no such thing as evil. He said some people just shouldn't marry each other was all. After a few weeks I stopped seeing the psychiatrist. I couldn't understand what he was talking about. Evil's real. I have it.

O'Connor had it too. That's one reason he was so gentle. He knew he could kill. He pretended to be good, with his basketball and his cowboy boots and his hairy nervous hands. He pretended to be too good to even hurt a fly; he saved things, women, flies. I used to watch him. I was wearing false eyelashes again; I watched him behind a fringe of clipped mink. He'd sit at the window strumming "Lay Lady Lay"—or something that sounded just like "Lay

Lady Lay"—and every now and then he'd stop, get a paper cup, cup it over a fly buzzing at the pane, open the window, and set the fly free. It annoyed me; I hated to watch his bent back and pious knees. Sometimes he damaged the flies saving them, broke their legs or tore their wings. That, I thought, was evil. And saying he'd been wrong about me, that I had no abilities at all, not even nice penmanship when you looked at it hard or knew something about handwriting analysis—that was evil. Touching my face, toward the end, not as if he were creating it with an airbrush but erasing it with a rag—that was evil. And pulling himself back from me, piece by piece, part by part, hand by foot by eye by lip, until nothing was left, not even imitations, until there was no one there—that was evil. Leaving me with no word of good-bye—that wasn't evil. That was justice. I deserved no good-bye.

One morning just before he disappeared O'Connor woke up and turned to me on the pillow. His eyes were bright and huge and beautiful. "I feel," he cried, "like a jar of emeralds!" And then he closed his eyes and pretended to go back to sleep and I pretended too, breathing lightly, scared to ask him what he meant, scared to know him. It was early and it was Sunday and we would have to spend the long day together, and after a minute or two we were both truly asleep, not pretending. I had a dream. I dreamt I was inside a dark room. I could see the moon through the curtains and I could hear someone breathing, light and quick, outside the front door. O'Connor, I thought. He wants to come in. I felt the wood hard beneath my hand and hard beneath my hip as I held that door shut. I'm only twenty-two, I thought in my dream. I have two marriages behind me, thousands to go.

Heart and Soul

J ohn and Joan Bartlett are driving north on a warm
winter morning to look at a piano John wants to buy.
Joan has packed a picnic lunch and a bottle of wine;
she has brought sweaters and a camera in case there
is snow. She hopes to see snow. She hopes to see mountains
and pine trees and a river with white rocks. She leans her
head on John's shoulder and looks out the window. They
have been driving for an hour and so far all she has seen are
a few orchard trees behind squat office buildings and a large
puddle of rain water, shining like silver, between two warehouse parking lots.

"Glad you came?" John asks. "Or would you rather be
at work?"

"Glad," Joan says. She shivers, thinking of work. She
types insurance forms for a large company. When she called
this morning to say she was sick, her supervisor hesitated,
as if she couldn't place Joan's name. "Still," Joan says, "I
hate to lie."

"Everyone lies," John says. Joan moves away slightly to
let him pull a dollar bill out of his wallet for the bridge toll.
She watches him smooth it on his knee. "I just hope this
old guy in Woodburn is telling the truth. If he is, we're
going to get a deal to end all deals. A grand piano for two
thousand dollars? I still can't believe it."

"Two thousand dollars?" Joan repeats. She hasn't heard

the price before. "That's a lot of money." She is in her ninth week of pregnancy and feels dazed all the time. She smiles and waits for John to explain. "Do we have two thousand dollars?"

John smiles back but does not answer. John handles the money now; that was a decision they made when they married. If Joan wants money, she has only to ask him. "Do we?" she asks again, and John nods and says, "We're doing all right." He slows at the toll gate, gives the man the dollar, and hands Joan the change. "Don't say I never gave you anything," he drawls.

"I would never say that," Joan replies simply. She holds the money in her palm a long time before slipping it into her pocket. John is still handsome, but he looks so much younger without his beard that he seems like a stranger. His face is paler now, and a little lopsided. She wishes he had quit his job—had just walked out the door—when his boss told him to shave last week. He would have, she's sure, if he hadn't been worried about her and the baby. She starts to put her head back on his shoulder, but stops as he leans forward to turn the car radio up.

"Listen to this," he breathes. "Glenn Gould. Can you hear him singing as he plays? Man. If I could play like that."

"You can," Joan says. "All you need is a decent piano." She pulls a blanket from the back seat, wraps it over her legs, and tries to glimpse the ocean through the tall gray bars of the bridge. John is as good a musician as Glenn Gould—better, because he writes his own music. John's songs are the most beautiful she has ever heard. They are love songs, but sad, and they make her feel like dancing and crying at the same time; it's a feeling she can't explain, even to John, who brushes her off when she tries to praise him. The songs are unfinished, he says. They need work. Part of the problem is his job—he hates working with those people at the bank—and part of the problem is the piano they rent, a green painted upright with a thin, sour sound. Once they find the right piano, John will be able to finish his songs, and he can record them, and sell them, and then he can quit work forever. Joan is secretly afraid he will leave her when this happens; he will meet another woman, someone smarter and prettier than she. Sometimes she sits in a trance over her typewriter at work, sick with jealousy, thinking about this other woman. She glances now at John as he conducts the last notes from the radio, his wedding ring striking time on the steering wheel. The piano they are going to look at today—what kind did John tell her it was? She can't remember. She presses the palms of her hands against her still-flat stomach to hold the baby safe inside. She hopes the baby will have John's brains and John's talents and John's dark good looks, and she hopes it will love her more than John does and comfort her when John leaves. "I love you," she says, when the music ends. She waits. "Do you love me?"

"I'd do anything for you," John says.

This is not the answer Joan wants but it will have to do. She looks out the window and asks again about the man who is selling the piano. "He said he was desperate?"

"That's what he said."

"Desperate," Joan repeats. She likes the sound of the word. "And he said he needs cash by the weekend? I wonder why."

John says nothing.

"Maybe he's being blackmailed," Joan suggests. "Maybe he needs to have heart surgery or maybe he's in love with a show girl."

"I think it's taxes," John says.

Joan wrinkles her nose and stares out the window. Gray fields slide toward low gray mountains; she can see no snow. She hopes something interesting will appear outside the window so she can think of something interesting to say, but all they pass are fields and housing tracts, fields and housing tracts. She is glad she will not have to live in a housing tract. Once John sells his songs, they will have a small house on a cliff overlooking the ocean; there will be a pony for the baby, and a kitchen with its own garden for her, and a studio, filled with sunlight, for John to compose in. There will be gabled windows and a beamed ceiling and there might, or might not—she hasn't decided—be a thatched roof. She thinks of the house they will have, and sleeps. When John says, "Here we are," she sits forward, dazed. She sees a sign saying "Welcome to Woodburn," and behind it a wide thoroughfare littered with fast-food outlets and auto repair shops. John lifts a creased piece of paper from the dashboard and asks her to read directions. The directions take them off the thoroughfare into a subdivision of ranch-style houses with gingerbread trim and scuffed, fenceless lawns. John slows before the last house on the block and parks. "Look," he says. "You can see the piano in the window."

Joan peers toward the house but cannot see the piano because a tall, disheveled man is coming down the pathway to meet them. He is wearing a ski sweater, filthy blue jeans, and tennis shoes; his stride is hasty and feminine and his voice, as he hails them, quavers so noticeably that Joan can see why John thought he was older.

"You must have brought this bad old foggy weather up north with you," he cries. "It's been clear as a bell here all week long." He shakes hands with John, wipes his palms down his jeans, and shakes hands with Joan. He introduces himself as Sutton—Joan is not sure whether that is his first name or his last name—and leads them quickly into the house. John turns to shrug at Joan over his shoulder. Joan smiles back. The change from the bridge toll jangles in her pocket.

The inside of the house is nicer than the outside, and Joan likes the braided rag rugs, maple furniture, and copper wall plaques. She stoops to pet a black cat asleep on the overstuffed sofa, and stops to admire a stained-glass parrot hanging from a wire at the window.

"I thought you said this was a grand piano," John says. His voice sounds loud in the quiet room, and Sutton, who is arranging stalks of dry weeds in a vase on the mantel, jumps a little.

"It is," Sutton says. He looks at Joan. "Isn't it?"

"I don't know," Joan begins, but John, in the same loud voice, interrupts.

"It's a baby grand," John says. "Your ad didn't say it was a baby grand. And when I spoke to you on the phone you didn't mention that either."

"Is there a difference?" Sutton stammers.

"We're going to have a baby," Joan says, as Sutton's eyes flit from her face to John's. It's a silly thing to say and she flushes. "We're going to have a baby in July."

"Five hundred dollars difference," John says. "At least."

"A Cancer?" Sutton says to Joan.

"Moon child," Joan nods back.

Joan and Sutton smile at each other as John sits down to play, but Joan's smile freezes as she realizes all John wants to play are scales, single notes that plod up and down the keyboard, and Sutton's smile disappears altogether when John looks up and says, "I can't understand why you've never had it tuned."

"Never tuned? Why it was tuned just last week!"

John shakes his head and gives a short, sad laugh. "Listen to this," he says. He plays a note that sounds all right to Joan. He plays it again and again. Sutton clucks his tongue and says, "Really. Just last week. I don't know what could have happened. The weather? Some change in the weather?"

"I doubt it," John snaps, and Joan flushes again, for him this time, for his rudeness, which she never expected. "It's a beautiful piano," she says, turning to Sutton. "A beautiful shape, isn't it, like a big violin, and such a pretty color. What kind of wood is it? Oak?"

Sutton scarcely looks at her as he answers. "It's mahogany," he says, jabbing a cattail down into the vase. "It's rare Philippine mahogany that's been stained to look like oak. I refinished it myself. Oh you should have seen it when I found it," he says, his voice rising as John hits one hard note after another. "It was just an old black box stuck off in a corner of this abandoned schoolhouse and when I saw it I knew, I just knew, right away I thought: This is a treasure. Has that ever happened to you?"

"Yes," Joan says, "it has." If she knew Sutton better she would tell him about the first time she saw John. John was playing in an outdoor wedding and he looked so hot and uncomfortable in his tuxedo, so out of place, really, with his beard and dark glasses, that she felt sorry for him. She brought him a bottle of champagne and one plastic cup. She was wearing her bridesmaid dress and as she turned to leave the stage she tripped on her hem and he caught her, and everyone clapped, and that's when she knew. But she doesn't know Sutton well enough to tell him about that yet, and besides she has lost his attention. His eyes are darting from John to the window to his own face in the mirror over the mantel.

"Everything is for sale," he says suddenly. "Everything in my house, so just name your price."

Joan nods uncertainly and looks around as Sutton gestures toward a lamp, a table, a bookcase filled with Japanese dolls.

"Here," Sutton says. "Here's a present. On the house." He picks up a book and places it in her hands, but just as she looks down at it, John bursts into the opening bars of

"Rainbow Chaser." Joan gasps with pleasure. This is her song, the one John wrote just for her. The room grows small around her as she listens, and then it peels away, leaving her alone and uplifted in some cloudy space spangled with little lights. She wants to sing out as the music swirls up from inside her and swirls back toward John. Tears blur her eyes and she takes a step toward the piano. John looks up, smiles past her briefly, and stops playing.

"That was beaut . . ." Joan begins, but Sutton, behind her, interrupts.

"Real cocktail lounge melody," he says.

Joan turns, stunned, but John laughs easily. "Yes," he says. "Yes it is. By the way, the second pedal is broken. I guess you knew? And the action is slow. Have you had it adjusted?"

Sutton moves to stare down at the keyboard as John demonstrates the slow action. Joan sits down by the black cat, but it swishes its tail when she pets it, so she pulls her hand away. Sutton is probably going to sell you next, she thinks to the cat. She looks down at the book in her hand; it's a picture book for children about a wishing well that gives and gives until it has nothing left. She slips the book back on the coffee table. She looks up to hear Sutton say, "But I told you on the phone I've already put over a thousand of my own money into it. And now you say you can only offer twelve hundred?"

The two men are standing by the window with their backs to her. Joan, who has not yet had a chance to inspect the piano at close range, slips into the vacated bench and looks at the lettering above the keyboard. It's an A. B. Chase. That's what John told her. Why couldn't she remember that? ABC. You don't have to be a genius to remember ABC. She drops her head and begins to pick out "Heart and Soul," which is the only piece of music she knows. She wishes John would just admit his offer is too low so they could leave and let Sutton try to sell the piano to someone who can afford it, but John keeps repeating the same sum, twelve hundred dollars, and the same phrase: Take it or leave it. "To tell the truth," John says now, "twelve hundred is all the money I have."

"*We*," Joan corrects softly from the piano bench. She has not meant to speak and the sound of her own voice surprises her. Surprised, she adds, in the same muffled voice, "And it's not all we have. We're doing all right. We have two thousand dollars."

John turns, stares at her steadily, and Sutton stares too—for a second their expressions, polite and blank, are so alike they might be father and son—then they both turn their backs to her again. "I shouldn't even be offering twelve hundred," John continues to Sutton. "I'm going to have to borrow money for the moving costs to truck the thing down to the city, and then I'm going to have to have that second pedal replaced and the action, God, I don't know. Having the action adjusted is not going to be cheap."

Joan plays "Heart and Soul" again, as much as she can remember, and then she sits and waits with her hands in her lap. She twists the diamond chip on her ring to catch the sunlight but there is no sunlight. He didn't, she reminds herself, actually ever say we had two thousand dollars; I just assumed he said it. I am always assuming things that aren't true.

"Joanie?"

She looks up, stands, lowers the lid on the piano, and trails after John and Sutton, who are still talking as they walk toward the car. The sky hasn't cleared but the air smells warm and springlike. "Is there a park in town?" Joan asks as Sutton opens the car door for her. "We thought we'd stop and have a picnic."

"There are parks galore," Sutton says. He gives a jaunty slam to the car door, followed by a jaunty wave. But the look on his face as Joan turns to wave back is one of rage, a tight flooded red look that makes her turn back toward John very quickly. John's expression isn't much better. "Just leave business to businessmen," John says. "You're not a businessman," Joan says, her voice low and stubborn. "You're a musician." "I was a businessman today," John says. He turns the corner, glances into the rearview mirror, hits the rim of the steering wheel with his palm, hollers "Whoopee!" and laughs out loud. "Best deal I ever made," he says. "Deal?" Joan repeats. "Weren't you listening? I bought it. We have a piano now." "You mean he sold you that piano for twelve hundred dollars after all?" "The guy's such a crook, Joanie. He's lucky to get that much. Trying to pass it off as a grand . . ." John shakes his head, still grinning. Joan, frowning hard, trying to get everything straight, says, "But isn't that piano too slow and too small for you? And the pedal . . . you can't record your songs if a pedal's broken. I don't know, John, I think you should hold out for a better piano, one you really love." "I love that one," John says. "It's perfect. It's rare and it's old and it's in fantastic condition." Well, good then, Joan thinks. That's settled. She leans back in her seat and wonders where they will put the piano, once they get it back to their apartment. It will take up the whole living room, but she can put it by the window and make pillows for the floor and maybe she can put a vase of dried weeds by the windowsill. She and the baby will play on the floor in the sunlight while John finds the final chords to "Rainbow Chaser" and sings to himself, under his breath, like Glenn Gould. "I figure we'll clear a thousand," John says. "More than that," Joan says. "That one song at least . . ." "I'm not talking about a song," John says. "I'm talk-

ing about the piano. After we get that piano down to the city I know I can get three thousand easy. Maybe more."
"We're going to sell the piano?"
"Sure. You didn't think we were going to keep it?"
Joan is too confused to even nod.
"With your company making you quit work three months before the baby's born? And my lousy salary?"
"But your songs . . ." Joan says.
"They'll just have to wait. Right now we need one thing and that one thing is money."

They cannot find a place for a picnic and at last John has to stop the car on a vacant lot by a construction site. The ground is scraped red and skeletal houses stand abandoned in the fog. A buzz saw drones in the distance and the car radio picks up nothing but static. Joan forgot salt for the hard-boiled eggs and she didn't bring a corkscrew for the wine, so they share a thermos of milk and pass the bag of cookies back and forth. Once John laughs out loud and she looks up, amazed at how homely he looks without his beard. He will never be famous, she thinks. He will never play on a stage for thousands of people, and no woman but me will love him. John sees her looking at him and touches the tip of her nose. "Penny for your thoughts," he says softly.
"I was thinking . . ." Joan begins. But she cannot go on. She has been wrong so often today; she might be wrong again. She moves over and rests her cheek against John's shoulder. She remembers how angry he was when he came home last week and shaved off his beard; she remembers how he threw his razor in the sink and hid his face in the towel so she would not guess he was crying. She said nothing then and she will say nothing now. She closes her eyes and touches his throat. She can feel him swallow and chew; she can feel the beat of his pulse. She puts her other hand on her own abdomen, wishing she could feel something from the baby too. But of course it's too soon to feel anything yet.

How to Quit Smoking

Norman's is the nicest bar. You can go in there alone without being bothered, and if you want to be bothered that's easy too. I like the cheese dip and the candles and the stained glass and the mirrors. The deep velvet sofas and overstuffed chairs make me feel at home. Since Bob and I split up I welcome a home, any home, and my special place at Norman's is in the corner by the fireplace. I can sit there and study and drink all night long.

I was reading Yeats the night I met Todd. I was drinking Irish coffees and dying for a smoke and Todd was standing at the bar talking to another girl. Right away I liked his clothes. He was wearing a dark blue suit and a paisley tie; he dressed the way Bob used to dress before Bob got so crazy, and I liked him for reminding me of Bob and for reminding me of Bob in a pleasant way, which has become increasingly difficult lately. So when the girl went to the john I put down my book and walked up to the bar and said, "Hey, I like your clothes," and he said, "Hey, I like yours too," and I had to laugh because I could tell he didn't. I was wearing the bowling shirt I'd bought at the flea market and the red rubber rain boots I'd found out by the trash. Todd said he especially liked the boots, and he dropped his eyes to them and looked up real slow, which is something that still makes me clench my fist and want to start swinging. But I can take it a little better now that

I'm older, and I'd already had two Irish coffees, which helped. When his eyes reached my necklace, I was prepared. I knew he'd want to pretend to touch it. "Teeth?" he said, his fingers brushing slowly across my skin. "Camel teeth," I told him. "I bought a whole set last summer when I hitchhiked through Egypt. My earrings are Alaskan dog bones." I lifted my hair. "Woof," said Todd. "You must get around." "I do," I assured him, and shook my hair down. "This year I've already been to Belize and Peru, and next week I'm leaving for Ireland."

Todd had never been to Peru, knew nothing about Ireland, and kept saying Woof, so after a few minutes I was ready to move on and talk to someone more lively. I would have, too, if Todd's fingers, lingering on my necklace, hadn't had such a heavy heat.

"You have an unusual body temperature," I said, surprised, and Todd said, "Oh yeah? How's that?" and turned his back to the girl coming back from the john, and after that we were together all night.

Aside from his physical warmth, though, there was nothing remarkable about Todd. He was a few years younger than I, with one of those cheeky faces and blow-dry haircuts you see downtown on all the baby businessmen. He told me he was a pilot and I told him I was a screenwriter; after another Irish he said he didn't actually have his pilot's license yet and I told him I hadn't actually finished a film script yet either. He said he worked in sales down the peninsula. I told him I went to Berkeley. I confessed I'd changed my major twice since my divorce and still didn't know if I wanted to go into economics or pre-law or stay and finish my graduate work in anthropology. "Oh shit," Todd said, "you're an intellectual." He rubbed his upper lip and glanced at himself in the mirror behind the bar. I didn't want to lose him but I didn't want to keep him either; I'm pretty tired of men who think if you read a book that doesn't have pictures you're a female Einstein, so I fished twenty cents out of my pocket and got up to try and find someone to sell me a cigarette.

"Smoking is the worst thing you can do to your body," Todd warned as I left, and I remembered Bob saying those exact words in that exact tone and it made me stop for a minute, puzzled. Smoking is a bad habit and one I hope to break very soon. But it certainly is not the worst thing you can do to your body.

"If I weren't so polite," I said to Todd, "I'd list you a dozen things that are worse."

The first smoker I found was a bald man in tennis shorts; he gave me two Marlboros and wouldn't accept the twenty cents as payment. "These are for your red rubber boots," he said. As I leaned forward for the match I felt Todd's hand on my back; it was like being touched with a warm little iron.

"Let's list those dozen," he said. He waved the smoke away from his face, watched me inhale, and sighed. "If you can't beat 'em," he said.

So I gave him a Marlboro and we settled back down by the fireplace. "This is the first cigarette I've had in five years," he said. "I smoked a lot when I was in Vietnam, did a lot of dope too, but now I drink. These are making me dizzy as hell. How can you stand them?"

I told him I only smoked a couple of cigarettes a day, which is about right, although since Bob and I broke up I guess I've been smoking more often. "Bob your husband?" Todd asked, and I told him no, I'd lost track of my husband; Bob was just this psychologist I got involved with when I started getting headaches, but Bob's problems were even worse than mine and after a while we drifted apart. "We were going to write a book together," I told

Todd. "We were going to rent a house in Puerto Vallarta and work on this book about displacement anxiety and his children were going to live with us too." Thinking of Bob made me turn to a man behind me and ask for the time; I'm supposed to go downtown one of these days and get the rest of my stuff before Bob puts it out on the street. But the time was too late for Bob's, and I stood. "I've got to head home now," I said. "Where's my book?"

"Home?" Todd said. He pried my Yeats from between the cushions on the couch, said, "Fairy tales?" and handed it back. "Where do you live?" he asked.

For a second I had to actually stop and think. I'd been moving around so much. My plants were at BJ's and my record player and cookbooks were at Blackie's, and my clothes, God, my clothes were in closets all over San Francisco. Bob had the good stuff, the African masks and the turquoise things and my model's portfolio. I'll have to get them next week, I thought, when I find out about the loan, because the minute that student loan comes through I'm leaving for Dublin. In Ireland I'll live in farmhouses, with families, and that will be nice—but tonight? Tonight? I stared into Todd's clear blue eyes.

"I live on Telegraph Hill," I said, remembering, with relief, that I'd been invited to stay with Bob's brother's friend Alex. "It's not a long walk. It's been a pleasure meeting you. Too bad you don't smoke."

"Walk?" Todd asked. "In the dark?"

"It's all right," I said, and it is. I have never been approached on the streets. Bob once said the anger in me was so obvious that all the rapists, thieves, and muggers out in the world would recognize me as one of them and leave me alone. This is typical of Bob's crazy theories. It's true about the anger, all right, and I was angrier when I was living with Bob than I've ever been in my life, but I think the main reason I've never been attacked is that I walk

very fast and I walk as though I know exactly where I'm
going, even though, most of the time, I do not.
"Didn't you see *Looking for Mr. Goodbar?*" Todd asked.
Everything about his rosy-cheeked face looking up from
the velvet sofa was annoying, but the question intrigued me.
Looking for Mr. Goodbar was a seriously flawed film, and I'd
been wanting to have a long talk about it with someone. But
Todd, it turned out, hadn't seen the film at all. He thought
it was about women who get punished for picking men up
in bars, so I kissed him gently on the top of his blow-dried
bangs and left. He caught up with me a block or two later.
"Since you're walking toward my car I'll just walk along
with you," he said. "You're a very independent little person, aren't you? Sort of cute. I like that. Come on, I'll give
you a ride."

He unlocked his car and when I saw what he drove I
couldn't resist; I had to say yes. A fabulous car, BMW,
burgundy, with fabulous upholstery. He opened the door for
me and as I slid in he patted my hip; I didn't care about
that and I didn't care when he put Rod Stewart on the tape
deck and started to sing along in a loud English accent either. I was delighted just to be sitting in a real car again,
with soft glove leather under my palms and that great male
scent all around me and the city slowly drifting past the
windows like lit scenes from a dream or a long dissolve in a
romantic film. When he parked in front of Alex's apartment
I thought that was like a movie too. In movies, parking
places always appear. "You ought to come in," I said.

Todd blinked. "Won't your friend Alex object if I do?"
he asked.

"I don't know Alex well enough to know what he'd object to," I admitted. "But you've had a lot to drink. You
ought to have a cup of coffee."

"I wouldn't mind some coffee," Todd said. He looked at
me and shook his head. "Peculiar little person," he said. He

came around and opened my door. A man watching from the sidewalk laughed. I laughed too. I was still thinking about film, and how we looked like a couple in a beautiful film, walking from our glamorous car toward our stylish apartment, when the same man, no longer laughing, stepped close and raised an enormous knife.

"Don't move," he said, "or I'll kill you."

"What?" I said. "Is this a joke?" But the man already had his elbow locked around Todd's throat and was bending him backwards. The knife shone against Todd's tie like a silver tie-clip, I thought, a huge ugly silver tie-clip. "Don't move, Todd," I cried, but just then Todd ducked and turned and there was a terrific struggle with both men swearing and making sounds like sobs and I just stood there with a stupid smile on my face, waiting for it to be over. I have always wondered how I would behave in a crisis, and now I know: I stand very still with my hands clasped; I stare. I still had the feeling I was watching a film. When Todd whirled around, clutching the knife in his own hands, I examined his face as calmly as I would any actor's, and it wasn't until the other man had run off into the darkness that I realized something had happened, really happened, to both of us. I touched Todd. His pale face. His incredible heat. Was it ebbing? Was he bleeding? I pivoted him around, checking for wounds with my hands. There were none. The blue suit was not slashed through the back; there was no blood on the shirt, no blood on the tie, no blood on the knife he finally let drop to the street.

Alex insisted on calling the police. The police were just another bother as far as I was concerned; I couldn't wait for them to leave. "I learned karate in Vietnam," Todd kept explaining in a loud shaky voice, but even as he described his karate to the police and even as the police made notes I was still checking his knees, his thighs, the backs of his arms, his round young face for the wounds. I could not, literally could not, keep my hands off him. The only thing I wanted more than touching Todd was another drink and a cigarette. While the patrol car drove us around the neighborhood to see if he could point out the attacker, I sat as close to Todd as I could, and when the car stopped to let us into an all-night market for Shermans and a bottle of gin, I plunged my hands into Todd's suit pockets and walked down the store aisles like that. I wanted to crawl down his collar and camp. Back at the apartment I sat on his lap.

Alex was uneasy watching us. He sipped his drink and patted his toupe and kept asking Todd if he felt well enough to drive home now—a question that I answered, quickly, "No! Not yet! Can't you see he's not ready yet?" Alex tried to make conversation about the influence of heroin addicts and homosexuals and southern blacks on crime in San Francisco, but when I started to undress Todd in front of him he flushed and left the living room at once. What could he do? I felt sorry for him. I felt bad about abusing his hospitality, but I was not myself. The attack had shaken me out of myself. I was trembling so hard I could hear my earrings click like fingers snapping as I stripped. My hands were too shaky to pull off the red boots. "Hold still," ordered Todd, and I laughed because I couldn't. "Hold still," he said again, and I tried, but even trying I was trembling. He threw the boots across the room and sat down on the floor. "I'm not in the mood," he said. I laughed again. With his hair all mussed and his clothes half-off he looked for the first time as if he'd been in a fight. "I can't," he said crossly, but I reached out and touched him. He felt warm, and solid, intact.

"Oh yes you can," I said. I knew he could. He had to. I couldn't hold still unless I held on, and he needed me to hold onto too.

So all that night we held tight to each other. It wasn't love we made, it was better than love, it was the best sex

I'd had since the first few times with Bob. We tumbled around that apartment like a couple of circus stars, tackling each other in room after room, leaving a trail of couch cushions and towels and camel teeth behind us. I was sobbing and singing and Todd was sweating and shouting and Alex was hitting the wall with his fist, but we couldn't be still yet, we still couldn't stop. Every time I closed my eyes I saw Todd and the other man fighting on the street, and when I opened my eyes I felt as if I was Todd and Todd was the man with the knife, or I was the man with the knife and Todd was me, watching the struggle. When the night was at its darkest and stillest we piled pillows beneath the window and, at last, lay still. We smoked the rest of the cigarettes then, and finished the bottle of gin. And we talked.

We talked about family, mostly. I don't know why. I told him about my grandmother, about her massive English furniture and her Italian houseboy and her ginger cookies and her sour powdery smell; I told him how much I had loved her. I started to cry. Todd rocked me back and forth on the floor as I cried; he was warm as bread dough and I cried a little more, liking the taste of my tears on his skin. Then he told me about his family, the sister with twin girls, the older brother who had made so much money, the father he couldn't talk to. He described the small town in Indiana where he'd grown up, and I could smell the cut grass when he described it, and see the flowering dogwood. Just before dawn he said he had to go home, and I realized he had said that before; he had wanted to go home even before Alex called the police.

"I can't let you go home," I said, my lips warmed by his skin. I was almost asleep. "You don't have a home."

"I have an apartment in Millbrae," he said, his voice high as a boy's in the dark. "You're the one who doesn't have a home."

But I held him and he stayed with me a little longer. When it was light I heard him washing in the bathroom; he used a lot of water and spat in the sink a long long time. He was as immaculate in his suit when he stepped out as he had been in Norman's the night before. "I'll call you," he said. "We'll have dinner. Go dancing."

He laughed unhappily and then he left. I walked around hugging myself after he left and then I walked around hugging two pillows and then I rapped on Alex's door but no answer there of course so I went through the ashtrays and picked out the longest butts and smoked until it was time to get dressed and hitch a ride into Berkeley. I thought: I will marry Todd and have his children, twin boys and twin girls. We will live in a beautiful house, furnished like my grandmother's, only out in the country. I fell asleep with a lit cigarette in my hand and woke up a second later with a bad burn on my thumb. Alex was already dressed, carrying my suitcase out to the street with precise little steps. "Bob was right about you," Alex said. "You're nothing but a whore."

Oh whore, whore, what a convenient word for men to use, and what do I care anyway? The only thing I cared about was Todd. I could think of no one else. I missed his heat; I missed his touch; I missed his tired voice in the dark. I telephoned from school and I telephoned again when I got back to the city. Todd said he couldn't talk. He said he had a call on another line and a lot of paper work to do. He said the paper work was piling up. At last he said it wasn't paper work at all. "It's my life," he said. He cleared his throat. "An incident like last night, well, it changes things. It puts a different light on things."

"What do you mean?"

"I mean I have a lot to think about right now. A lot to sort out."

"Can't I help you think?"

"No, you can't. Look. Tell you what. I'll call you."

"I don't have a phone," I reminded him, but he said, "The thing is, right now I have to be alone."

"Alone?" I repeated. "Why would you want that?"

"I just do," he said, and hung up.

Still, when I got to Norman's later on I thought I'd try just one more call. I stowed my suitcase under a mahogany table with clawed feet like one my grandmother had in her hallway, and I carried my Yeats and my Guinness out to the phone booth.

"Again?" Todd said. "Look, you're a generous and spunky girl and I appreciate everything you tried to do for me last night, but you've got to learn one thing. You've got to learn when to quit." He sucked his breath in. "You just don't quit."

He paused. I looked out through the phone booth at the late afternoon sun falling on Norman's; I could see the dirt on the floor and the stains on the upholstery and the acne on the bartender's downcast face. I wondered what the pubs in Dublin would be like, and if I'd still get headaches there. A girl walked by me. I grabbed her sleeve and made cigarette gestures with my two fingers against my lips. She gave me an Old Gold and lit it. I inhaled deeply and turned back to the phone, even though the phone, as I knew, would be dead. The cigarette felt so little in my hand then, slim as a baby bird bone. I thought, What if someone were hanging off a cliff and someone else tried to reach them but instead of offering a hand or a rope they just held out a cigarette, well that wouldn't work, the person would fall. I replaced the receiver and, turning, felt a cool kiss on the top of my head. Looking up I recognized Walter, Bob's old hypnotist.

"Still smoking?" Walter said. "I could cure you of that disgusting and repulsive habit in three free sessions if you want."

"Free?" I said.

"Well, not exactly free," Walter said, and smiled. But as I turned to leave he took his mirrored sunglasses off and rubbed his eyes and he looked so pale and saggy I asked what was the matter. "Drinking too much. Not eating right," Walter said. He sighed. Then he told me that he'd never forgotten the night Bob asked him for dinner and I cooked fried chicken with gravy and green beans braised with bacon and baking powder biscuits and deep-dish apple pie. "Do you still cook that good way?" he wanted to know. I shrugged. I'm a good cook, and I'll cook any way, home-style or free-style, whatever they want. "I want a good dinner," Walter explained, and so we bargained for a while and finally I said I'd cook him the best dinner he'd ever eaten in his life if he'd help me quit smoking and he said, "Agreed." Because Todd was right. I've never known how to quit and I've tons of bad habits I ought to give up.

"I want to change my whole life," I told Walter, and he raised his champagne glass and clinked it to mine.

"You've come to the right man," he said, and laughed and licked his lips. When we finished the bottle I picked up my suitcase and followed him home.

Baby Pictures

The light's right, bright as foil, a long silver sheet rolling in through the east kitchen window. I take one look and race back to the bedroom. "Mama?" Wynn calls as I pound past his door. "Mama? It's up time?"

"One second," I tell him. I find the camera where I left it, on top of the laundry. I snatch at it fast and race back to the kitchen. The light is still there, and everything blazes: the toaster, the step stool, the pears set to ripen on the sill. The dishes Robert left piled in the sink are the loveliest things I've ever seen in my life. I clamp the camera to my eye and hold my breath. The soiled plates, crushed napkins, and empty wine glasses burst into focus, each edge as sharp as if carved from a mirror. I lean forward, add Wynn's battered cup, subtract one gutted white candle, lean back, smile. It's going to be good. I steady the camera, touch the shutter—and just as I do, the back door flies open and Leslie Carney's shadow leaps over my shoulder to darken the drainboard. I turn with both hands raised. "Don't shoot me," Leslie giggles.

"Don't tempt me," I warn her. She's gleaming with sweat from her morning run, her face flushed, her hair stuck to her forehead.

"I knocked," she says. "You just didn't hear me. I had to come over. I've got the best news. You won't believe it."

What I won't believe, I think, as I lower the camera, is how little it takes to lose a good shot. I sigh at the sink of soiled dishes—ordinary plates in ordinary daylight—and set the camera down. Leslie pulls a yellow leaf from her sweat shirt pocket, hands it to me, and grins at my bathrobe. It's a long red Chinese robe with a torn hem and a grass stain on the knee; it was made in Paris and lined in silk, and despite Leslie's grin I can tell she admires it. Leslie is a jeweler; she too works at home, and she would give anything, I know, to have a robe of rich red silk to work in. I wear this robe for that—for making my pictures—and because I am pregnant again and need clothes that are loose.

"I'd like champagne," Leslie says, "but it's eight in the morning so I'll settle for tea. What kind do you have? Anything with rose hips is fine. I like rose hips when I've got cramps and oh man do I have cramps. I've got my period. My wonderful period. Two weeks late but I've got my period."

"That's your news?"

"That's part of my news."

"Leslie's here," Wynn sings from the bedroom. "Up time, Mama. Breakfast for Wynn time."

"I mean, I don't want to sound tactless," Leslie says, watching me put a pot of water on to boil for tea, "but if I were pregnant again right now I would kill myself. If I had to start over and do what you do all day, I'd never have time for myself." She follows me down the hall to Wynn's room, her voice a light hiss at my heels.

Wynn has taken the pillowcase off his pillow and put it over his head. Since he is wearing nothing else, the effect is predictable, and Leslie, whose own children are ten and twelve and girls besides, stares at him sorrowfully and says, "See. I just couldn't take it." I scoop Wynn's damp pajamas and diapers from under the mattress where he has stuffed them, toss them toward the hamper, grab jeans and shirt from half-opened drawers, and carry him, kicking and singing, masked and naked, back into the kitchen.

"No bath?" he asks, from beneath the pillowcase. "No bath today?"

"Later," I tell him. "He hates to have his hair washed," I explain to Leslie.

"They all do," Leslie says. I let it pass. Leslie is my age but acts like she's older. She's been married longer and had children earlier and seems to have always known what she wanted to do with her life. I feel as if I'm just beginning to find out. I started taking pictures five years ago—about the same time I met Robert—and I had my first, and last, exhibit the month before Wynn was born. It's hard, Leslie has told me, to handle marriage and children and career— hard, but not impossible. Leslie herself has lived in the same house with the same man for fourteen years, and she has worked on her jewelry steadily through pregnancies, breast-feedings, childhood illnesses, Scout troops, and orthodontists' appointments. If she can do it, I tell myself, so can I. I lift the pillowcase off Wynn's head and contemplate his rosy face.

"He threw up last night," I explain to Leslie. "In his crib. I didn't give him a full bath then because it was late and the tub was full of my trays and equipment."

"You need your own darkroom," Leslie says, shaking her head. "I've told you and told you . . ."

"He hasn't thrown up since," I interrupt. "I hope it's not flu."

"Lara used to throw up all the time when she was two," Leslie says. "It's their digestive systems. They aren't developed yet."

"Digestive systems," I repeat, impressed. Wynn, bouncing, singing, lets me dress him, then slips off my knees, runs into the living room, turns on the TV, and plumps down to a babble of cartoons. I am aware of Leslie's disapproval (she does not own a TV) and I feel that disapproval deepen as she watches me wander around the kitchen fixing Wynn's breakfast. The dry cereal, I realize, has too much sugar, the milk is not nonfat, the juice is not fresh-squeezed. Leslie contents herself with a brief sigh and starts to touch her toes. I carry Wynn's breakfast in to him, set it down and kiss him softly on top of his head. His hair smells foul and as soon as Leslie leaves I'll start his bath. I dread it already. He'll fight. He'll hit me and scream. I'll scream and hit back. We'll both be drenched with bath water, struggling, slipping, cursing, he on his knees in the water, me on my knees on the tiles, both of us shouting "Stop it!", both of us in tears, neighbors phoning police, an axe splitting the door, sirens, trained dogs, a reporter calling Robert at the office.

Leslie is doing leg lunges when I come back in, her short solid body posed like an archer's in the doorway. "She's not like your other friends," Robert said when he met her. "She isn't crazy and she isn't pretty." I was surprised that Robert, usually so astute, could not see Leslie's beauty. Perhaps he's never noticed her eyes. They are small and half-hidden under the thick blonde bangs she forgets to clip back, but they are beautiful eyes, shy, quick, and as luminous as the moonstones she works with. She works with ebony, ivory, and opals too. She designs bracelets and breastplates—big heavy pieces—Amazon armor. She told me once, without smiling, that she was developing a personal mythology, based on her study of the goddess Artemis. I answered, unsmiling, that I knew what she meant. My goddess has neither name nor mythology, but I wait on her too, and watch for her blazing. Leslie straightens now and pats her flat stomach.

"You know what I'd be doing today if I hadn't gotten my period?" she asks. "I'd be at the clinic, waiting in line for an abortion. Carney would be in line behind me, with a gun at my back. You know how he is. The last thing he wants is a baby right now." Leslie assumes I know her husband better than I do, but in fact I've only met him once. Carney is a contractor who came to our house, alone, to talk about building a darkroom for me. I remember a slight, soft-spoken man in a baseball cap. There was nothing distinctive about him, and if I were to pass him on the street without his cap I would not be sure enough to say hello. Sometimes Leslie wears his cap when she rides her bike, but I always know Leslie, in all her disguises. I recognize her in her blue jeans, in her sweat suit, in the long lace dress she wears to the art fairs. I recognize her at the market, on the schoolyard, in front of the post office. We meet, I sometimes think, like spies; we hide behind our grocery bags the way spies hide behind newspapers. We stand in broad daylight and exchange secrets. We know all the passwords. Our password is "He."

"He," Leslie says now, "already made me have one abortion. Best thing he ever made me do, too." She takes the cup of tea I pour her and sits down at the table. "So," she says. "You've traveled all over. What's a good place to stay in New York?"

"New York? Who's going to New York?"

She grins. "Remember that craft show I applied for? Well, they took me. I got the letter yesterday. They liked the slides I sent—especially the series of winged headbands. They said my work was just what they were looking for. Man! Can you believe it?"

"Yes!"

We are shrieking and laughing across the table. "I'm so excited," Leslie cries. She claps her hands over her eyes. "But what do you think I should do?"

"Do? What do you mean? You should go."

"What if Carney won't let me?"

"Won't *let* you?"

"What if he tries to stop me?"

I laugh again. Leslie does not. Pouring my own tea, I say, "How can he stop you?"

"He broke my arm once."

I look up, shocked. Leslie shrugs. "I don't think he meant to. Some guy was coming on to me, once, at an opening; Carney thought I was flirting or something. He's kind of insecure lately. So he's not going to like the idea of me flying off for a week in New York."

"You mean you haven't told him yet?"

"I've been thinking I may never tell him. Until the night before I leave." She drops her eyes, stirs her tea. Wynn hollers, "More toast," and as I get up to make it I say, "You could take Carney with you."

"I can't afford his ticket. As it is, I'm going to have to use money he doesn't even know about. This friend of mine—this lawyer I met at the tennis courts—he helped me set up a special account. In my maiden name. Carney can't touch it."

I'm thinking what I'd give for a week with Robert in New York, but I don't say that. One of the best years of my life was spent with Robert in New York; we were starting out and everything was free and easy between us. We were determined to be different from other couples we knew—we were going to be kinder and smarter and more successful. We were never going to fight and we were going to share everything—dreams and responsibilities—equally. I block the breadboard so Leslie can't see me putting marmalade on Wynn's toast, and then I carry it in to him. When I come back to the kitchen I see that Leslie is leafing through a book of Imogene Cunningham's photographs on the table.

"What's your favorite?" she asks me.

"Favorite? That's hard. Maybe this one . . ." I open the

book and point to a picture of an unmade bed, all soft folds
and shadows. "I love this one. When Cunningham's children were little she did what I'm trying to do now—that is,
she took pictures of things around the house and garden.
Some of her best work was done when she was a housewife." I smooth my bathrobe over my belly, feeling the
baby move, as I stare down at the picture. "It can be
done," I say. I follow Leslie's speculative look toward the
dishes in the sink, and laugh. "Those," I dismiss them,
"those are Robert's. It was Robert's night last night. He
was supposed to wash up but he forgot."

"Men don't do a damn thing," Leslie says.

I take a deep breath. "He," I say, "was supposed to
watch Wynn and do the dishes last night so I could go to a
lecture at the college. When I came home I found Wynn
asleep in his crib with vomit on his blanket. Robert hadn't
even undressed him. His shoes were still on."

Leslie shakes her head. We have finished our tea, but I
don't make more. Thinking of Robert's laziness has made
me lazy. Thinking of Robert's selfishness has made me want
to withhold. I'm remembering how Robert tricked me into
making love to him last night when I came home; that's
what I cannot forgive—that he fooled me into all the old
exhilaration, then let me pad by myself into our child's
room, stretching, smiling in wifely content, to discover
there the sort of man I'd married. I was angry last night
and I'm angry today. Anger feels almost natural now, to me
and to Robert too; we take it for granted, accept it as an
everyday mood. We no longer think of ourselves as a couple
set apart. "His accounts . . ." I explain. "He said he had
to work on his accounts and since I had 'so much free time'
today . . ."

"Free time," Leslie repeats. She laughs. "The only time
I feel free," she says, "is when I'm alone." Her words
seem to surprise her, for she bends to tie her shoelace. I

notice her left hand is bare. She told me once she had never liked her wedding ring; Carney had picked it out for her. "And you know Carney's taste." She straightens, drums her fingers on her knees, and says, "Men are such babies."

Wynn, at the sound of the word "babies," comes running in and climbs on my lap. He sticks his tongue between his teeth and gets an absorbed, stupid look on his face as he starts to pull the front of my bathrobe open. "Don't do that," I warn him.

"Want to," Wynn says.

"No."

"*Want* to."

"It's hard when they're little," Leslie says. "You'll have more freedom next year." She turns to Wynn. "You be nice to your mother."

Wynn says, "No! *You* be nice!" He is about to say more when he hears the music of a favorite commercial. He gives me a brilliant smile, slips off my lap, and runs back to the television.

"Of course next year," Leslie continues, "you'll have the new one." She stands. "I've got to get going. Finish my run. I do twenty-five miles a week now. It's really amazing how strong I've grown." For a second I'm afraid she is going to make me feel one of her muscles, but her eyes are on the floor and her face looks sad. "I feel better than I ever have in my life," she says, "and the better I feel and the stronger I feel, the more restless I get. I can't explain it. I just feel . . . restless."

I know she is talking about sex. I am silent.

She sits down again, jiggles her knees up and down, and says, "The other night Carney and I were fooling around on the couch and I wrestled him down to the floor. You should have seen his face. Nothing like that had ever happened to him before in his life. He was so surprised. But he liked it too. Men like strong women. Just so long as they know they're still stronger." She throws me a knowing woman-to-woman smile that fades very fast. "When Carney and I were first married I couldn't drive a car. I couldn't balance a checkbook. I had to ask him for every cent before I went to the store. Now I do it all. I pay the bills and fix the car and put in the garden and he's just, you know, the same old Carney. Losing his hair. Getting a paunch. I feel sorry for him in a way. But I can't stop growing. I can't go backwards. I have to go forward. What else is there?"

She is looking at me, expecting an answer. "Well . . ." I begin. I don't know how to finish. There is the second in between backwards and forwards that sometimes blazes and can sometimes be captured. But I can't explain that.

"It's not fair," she says flatly. "Someone's always losing. You can't gain something without someone else losing." She picks the yellow leaf off the table, pulls it apart. "The other day," she says, "I was talking to this guy, this lawyer, and he was telling me about a trail ride you can take, up into the Sierras, you rent your own horse, and I thought, Oh man, wouldn't I love to get away. Just get up and go, all by myself."

We are both silent. We are both imagining the Sierras, the high dry sunlit air, the buzzing of bees, the flight of an eagle, the scent of sugar pine and smoke. I will take my camera, I think, and a knapsack of film. I will spend one day on clouds, one day on reflections, one day on . . . "Mama," Wynn sighs. He stands before me, aims, throws a toy car at my foot. It strikes and burns my ankle. "Thanks a lot," I tell him. He ducks his chin down. I can tell he is sorry. He doesn't like having Leslie here so early. He likes me to himself in the mornings. I like me to myself in the mornings too. "I want to get away," I say. There's a twitch to my voice—the anger that's become so familiar. "I want to get away and finish my portfolio. Do you know what's in my portfolio?"

Leslie shakes her head.

"Baby pictures," I say.

We both laugh. I think of my pictures: Wynn an hour old, a day old, a month old, a year . . . Wynn with Robert in the garden, at the beach, his arms around Robert's neck as Robert studies his accounts at the table . . . Wynn in a basket, a backpack, a walker, on foot . . . baby pictures. And although the baby changes in each one, turns into someone new who turns into someone else again, although the stately infant in lace becomes the radiant, skinny-legged shouter on the trike, although nothing has been lost or gained that I haven't caught, or tried to catch, at the instant of passing, although I have done my best, baby pictures they are, and remain. Leslie is right to treat me as someone younger, someone who still has a great deal to learn.

"Your time will come," Leslie promises. "Just hang on in. And oh, by the way, I have those earrings you wanted me to make for your mother-in-law. They're good. She'll like them."

"How much will you let me have them for?" I know Leslie's work is expensive, but she's already said she will give me a break.

"Money?" she says. "Let's see. I hadn't thought about money. You took those slides for me . . . let's say eighty."

"Dollars?"

"They'd sell for twice that at any gallery."

Too much, I think. Leslie and her husband both ask too much. Carney wanted a fortune to build the darkroom. Robert shook his head when I gave him the price. "You'll have to wait a little longer," Robert told me. But can I wait a little longer? I haven't sold a photo in over six months. At night I wake up wide-eyed, frightened. I listen to Robert breathing beside me; I get up and check on Wynn in his crib. I walk back and forth through the house in my bathrobe. I should take pictures then, in the dark; I should start a new series on insomniac housewives. Ghostly refrigerators, moonlight on mirrors, a bag of onions beginning to sprout. Leslie has told me she used to wake up too; she used the time to research Artemis.

She is explaining that gemstones are expensive as she clears off the teapot, rinses it, and sets it on the counter to dry. She tells me she uses only the finest materials. She tells me she has high standards and always manages to meet them. I know this. I approve. The little rabbit tails on her tennis socks flick as she paces around my kitchen. If I'm not interested in quality . . . if I want cheap stuff . . . "Leslie," I sigh. She subsides.

"I just don't want you to think I'm ripping you off," she mutters. "If you don't want to take them, someone else will."

"Let me think about it," I say. But I'm thinking that eighty dollars will make a good start toward building a darkroom. I walk Leslie to the door and watch her drop into her leg lunge again. The sun is strong as bleach now, stripping her hair, making her face, as she lifts it, shiny and tired. "I shouldn't have had that tea," she says. "It's going to slow me down. But thanks anyway." She turns, pauses, grins over her shoulder. "Where did you find that bathrobe again?"

"Paris," I tell her. "My first gift from Robert."

She groans and waves and I wave too as she jogs from sight. Then I close the door and look around the kitchen. I have to clean. I have to cook. I have to shop. I have to dress. I have to make one beautiful picture and then another and then a portfolio of beautiful pictures. But all I do is stand by the kitchen sink, eating crusts of toast off Wynn's

breakfast plate, staring at the leaves falling onto the patio. I
am remembering the last time I went to Leslie's house. We
sat on the floor of her studio, surrounded by tools neatly
nested in marked boxes, sunshine pouring in on everything,
alchemizing even the smell of burnt metals into an essence
airy, pure; we drank wine with our sandwiches and laughed
because we were so lucky, because we had it all, home and
husbands and children and good health and our own good
work to do too. I turn from the sink. Wynn has been
watching from the doorway. A shaft of mid-morning sun
falls on his hair.

"Is it later yet?" he asks, and I know at once he means
bath, is it time for the bath, time for our struggle.

"Not yet, my love."

"I don't like later."

"I don't like it either. I like now."

"What's now?"

"This."

I reach up, lift the camera off the top of the refrigerator
where I left it, uncap the lens, and focus on Wynn. I catch
him as he turns, hair filthy and on fire in the sunlight, already shouting, half-gone, in flight.

Chocolate Footballs

Joan is only twenty-four, but she already has a wrinkle, a thin line like a crack in her forehead. Lines are forming at the corners of her eyes as well. Her hair is darker since she had Jeffie and it doesn't curl like it used to; perhaps she should cut it? Find a new style? There are white spots on her fingernails she never had before, and of course the stretch marks, still purplish, after more than a year, and her nipples turned brown. There is a pimple on her chin and another one coming in high on one cheek. "I look too ugly to go to the store," she says.

John glances up from the television set. "Don't be ridiculous," he says. "You're not ugly. You're beautiful."

Joan sighs heavily and writes "milk" on the grocery list in her lap; she acts as if John's praise means nothing when it is in fact the one thing that sustains her. The word "ridiculous" bothers her—she does not understand why John had to say that—but the word "beautiful" is just what she wanted. She has not been sure whether John still thinks so or not. They have been married almost three years and there have been times lately, since the move to this new apartment and John's new job, when she has felt that he is ignoring her. He has not been rude, exactly; he has just not paid attention. It seems his attention is always diverted toward something else—the radio playing in the next apartment, a bit of food on Jeffie's bib, some story his friend Larry told him in a bar after work. These last few months John has been more interested in football than anything else. He watches TV every weekend, sitting on the floor in the beanbag cushion chair Joan made for his birthday, chain-smoking Marlboros and talking to himself, shouting really, yelling things like "Allllll right!" and "Stomp them!"—things that seem, to Joan, borrowed. She can hear Larry talking like this, but John is gentler, more sensitive than Larry; his shouts are the shouts of a fraud, a bad actor. She and John have joked about this; he has told her that he learned to shout at a television, as he learned to fix flat tires and fix the kitchen drain, at Male School, a private place with a secret curriculum, no girls allowed. He whistles at the TV now, and Joan, who has never learned to whistle, says, "Is it over?" and in the next beat, "Do you love me?"

The question shames and obsesses her; she asks it in her lowest voice and writes "bread" under "milk," intent on John's answer.

"I adore you," John says, his eyes on the screen. Joan feels her wrinkle deepen. It is an anxiety line, the Avon lady has told her, and anxiety lines cannot be camouflaged by foundation or powder, removed by massage, or erased by creams. "A young girl like you?" the lady had asked her. "What do you have to worry about?" And Joan, with Jeffie in her arms, had almost burst into speech, had almost told that tired-eyed, over-rouged, incurious stranger everything. My husband doesn't like me, he'd rather be with his old friend from high school, he never helps with the baby, we never go out, he used to play the piano, we used to talk, now nothing happens, he hates his job, it's the third job he's had, he can't stand his boss, he comes home depressed, you know how men are, they take it out on their wives, I'm alone all day, we just moved here, no friends . . . Joan can imagine complaining to strangers and the temptation shocks her. It's not as if she has anything real to complain about. John doesn't beat her. He is as tender and solicitous as ever. He's just distant. Silent. He has told her that it's not as easy for him to talk about his feelings as it is for her, and Joan believes this is true. When he does talk about his feelings he uses words—like "adore"—that she cannot altogether comprehend, words that do not seem real, somehow. She looks up and frowns at the group of gray and white men struggling on the television screen. "Is this the team that's going to play in the Super Bowl?" she asks.

"This is the pre-game," John says, as if that were an answer. "Did you write down beer?"

Joan unfolds the list. Larry is coming to watch the Super Bowl with John tomorrow, and Larry likes beer. "Yes," she says. "I guess I'll leave Jeffie with you while I shop. He's been taking such long naps lately. I remember one of the teachers at Whitney had a baby boy that took really long naps and it turned out the baby had a tumor. In the brain."

"Beer," John repeats. "Two six-packs. Don't forget."

"I'm not that absentminded," Joan protests, but John doesn't answer. She drives to the store, buys ground beef and the beer and of course *is* as absentminded as John thinks she is, for the date she writes on her check is 1966 and it has been 1967 for over two weeks now; she corrects the date and initials it and hopes the clerk will not notice. To hide her embarrassment she picks up a magazine and reads as she waits in the checkout line. The magazine shows models in silver boots and cheerleaders' skirts throwing balloons to each other on a football field. Joan studies the hair on one of the models. It is short and shiny and cut on a slant that falls over the forehead. She refolds the magazine and puts is back on the rack; she is still thinking about the haircut when the grocery clerk says, "Your change?

Ma'am? Don't forget your change." Startled, Joan holds
out her hand. She remembers this same clerk teasing her
about her age when she bought a carton of cigarettes for
John two weeks ago. Has she turned into a "Ma'am" in
two short weeks?

She carries the groceries out to the car, puts them in,
adjusts the rearview mirror to back the car up, and sees
instead her own still-startled face which seems, as she studies it, not so terribly bad . . . broad, pinkish, freckled,
lined . . . but with a new haircut? Driving home she sees an
empty parking place in front of the House of Beauty and on
impulse she takes it. She sits in the car for a moment, drumming her fingers on the steering wheel, but another glance
in the rearview mirror convinces her. She has heard about
the House of Beauty from the Avon lady; it is supposed to
be the best shop outside the city. "You probably can't take
me without an appointment," Joan begins, but the owner
himself, Mr. Doug, bald, tan, with gray unblinking eyes,
motions her off to a chair right away. His two o'clock cancelled, he says; she's in luck.

Joan, holding her purse in her lap, leafs through the
stack of magazines by the chair, trying to find the one with
the model in it. She can't find it, but her description seems
to satisfy Mr. Doug, for he nods knowingly as she talks. She
sits with a pink plastic apron around her shoulders, avoid-
ing her reflection as Mr. Doug cuts. She has never known
what to say to hairdressers and has found it best, particularly when they might be queer, to say nothing at all; she
might hurt their feelings. "I drive by your shop every day,"
she murmurs after much thought, and Mr. Doug nods
again, bending around her with his small silver scissors,
telling her when to lean to one side, when to lean to the
other. Her hair slides unseen to the floor. Her head, without
it, begins to feel cold and small and stylish. She imagines
how pleased John will be when he sees her with the new,

sleek, slanted bangs; she will have his complete attention tonight, his old possessive ardor. And Larry, a bachelor, will be surprised too; he might even fall in love with her a little—just a little, Joan amends, for although Larry is her husband's best friend she has never found him the least bit attractive. She bows her head when Mr. Doug asks her to, but the bite of an electric razor on her neck makes her jump and she says, "What are you shaving my neck for?"

"To give you a smoother line," Mr. Doug explains.

"The girl in the picture . . ." Joan begins.

"You want a smooth, clean line," Mr. Doug says, "around the neck." Joan looks up at her reflection and gasps. Her hands fly to her ears, which seem enormous, exposed, and red on her small cropped head. She remembers John joking when Jeffie was first handed to him in the hospital, "Thank God he got my ears, not my wife's . . ." Tears fill her eyes so fast she can scarcely see as Mr. Doug hands her a mirror and swivels her in the chair, but even blinded by tears she can tell it's all wrong. The hair is so short in back she can't pinch a finger full, and the nape of her neck looks white and mannish. The only good thing about the cut is the way the bangs fall over her forehead, covering her wrinkle, but even as she notices this one advantage Mr. Doug swivels the chair around, sweeps the forelock up, and hacks it off. "Oh no," says Joan. "For the sporty look," says Mr. Doug. He puts his scissors down and stalks away. It occurs to Joan he is having a breakdown of some sort. Trembling, she pays his receptionist, a tired looking woman with red fingernails who says, "You have a nice shaped head for that youthful style. Not everyone can wear it."

Joan drives home crying and is crying still when she opens the door. For once she is too upset to be oppressed by the gray light, the sparse canvas furniture, the smell of rug shampoo and ammonia from the diaper pail. The television is still on and John is changing Jeffie on the floor before it.

Jeffie sees her first. He laughs and says, "Boo." John looks up then, smiles, then laughs out loud, then sobers. "You had your hair cut," he says.

"Yes," says Joan. "What do you think?"

"Well," John says, "it's short."

"No," Joan says, "what do you really think?"

"I hate it," John says.

"I hate it too," Joan flares.

"Then why'd you let the guy do it?"

"I didn't let him do it. He did it by himself."

"Didn't you tell him how you wanted it cut?"

"I did tell him. He didn't listen."

"Larry's not going to recognize you when he comes over tomorrow."

"Who cares about *Larry?*"

John sets Jeffie on his feet, pats him lightly on the bottom, and lights a cigarette. He does not look at Joan.

"Do you really hate it? Do I look ugly?"

"You could never look ugly, Joan."

"Do you think I look ugly?"

There is a long pause while John smokes. At last he says, his eyes on the television, "You just don't look like yourself."

Joan does not feel like herself. She moves in a daze. She serves the dinner, does the dishes, plays cars on the floor with Jeffie. All the time the word "ugly" tolls in her head like a dull gray bell. She has felt ugly . . . she has often said she is ugly . . . but she has never actually *been* ugly before in her life. She tries to surprise a reflection from every surface that shines: her coffee spoon, the breadbox, the hilt of Jeffie's toy pistol. Every reflection says *ugly.* She wonders what it must be like to be maimed or crippled or in some way handicapped; she thinks she understands a little what that must feel like now. John watches TV, goes to bed without saying goodnight, and falls asleep reading *Sports Illus-*

trated. Joan decides to spend the night on the couch. She lies awake, her eyes on the ceiling, listening to the traffic from the freeway and the sound of untroubled voices from other apartments. She cannot sleep. After an hour she goes upstairs and gets into bed beside John and lies there stiffly, hoping he will accidentally touch her so she can move away, but John is deep in sleep and does not stir. He could have lied, she thinks. He could have lied to make me feel better. She cries a little before falling asleep. The last thing she feels is the wrinkle, setting itself deeper across her plain face. The next morning she awakens to find John staring down at her, his own dark hair ruffled and crested around his forehead.

"It will grow," he tells her.

Joan does not know what he is talking about.

"Your hair," he reminds her. "Your hair will grow back and you'll look like you used to."

"I thought you didn't like the way I looked before."

"Honey. Listen. I like any way you choose to look."

"Even this?"

"Even this."

"Then why were you so mean?"

John is astonished. "I wasn't mean," he says. "You were the one who was angry last night."

Joan supposes, on reflection, this is true.

"Snap out of it," he urges. "This is going to be a big day. Super Bowl Sunday." He kisses her nose and later, as he's coming out of the shower and she's feeding Jeffie in the high chair, he kisses the naked back of her neck. "Will you watch the game with us?" he asks. Joan, who had meant to stay in the bedroom reading a novel all day, is flattered.

"I'd love to," she says. John finishes feeding Jeffie while she gets dressed. She puts on a black turtleneck, black jeans, lots of eye makeup, and big hoop earrings; the earrings, she decides, make the haircut look French. She hopes

Larry will not try to say anything funny; she hopes today he
will leave her alone. She opens the door before he can finish
his rat-a-tat knock.

"Hi, Jane, Jean, Janet, sweetie, look, I brought you
some candy."

Joan takes the white paper bag and looks inside. It is
filled with tinsel-wrapped chocolates in the shape of little
footballs. "Chocolate footballs?" John exclaims, peering
over Joan's shoulder. "What a great idea! Where'd you
ever find chocolate footballs?"

Joan chimes in, wonderful, what an original idea, but
she is not sure. She does not trust Larry. The last time he
came over he told her he needed her help with a magic trick
he'd just learned; he could pull an egg through the crack in
the front door if Joan would just come around and put her
fingers through the opening, there, just below the hinges,
and hold the egg, like so, between her thumb and first finger, and there Joan had stood, gripping a raw egg she
didn't dare drop, for almost five minutes while Larry leaned
against the stairway, too weak with laughter to even move.
She remembers this and looks from the bag of candy to
Larry's flushed, jocular, smooth-shaven face. He winks and
says, "You've heard about chocolate footballs, Stud?"

"No," John says, smiling.

"Marriage is rotting the gray matter, Stud. Joan probably knows about chocolate footballs and just hasn't told
you."

"No," Joan says.

"Let me tell you about those footballs," Larry says. He
lowers his voice, speaking to John, and the two men pass,
laughing, into the living room. The television is already on
and as Joan pours the candy into a glass dish she hears the
beer being opened and the clink of two cans. It's not Larry,
she tells herself again, it's the way John acts around Larry;
he acts like a little kid and not like a grown man with a wife

and a child. She gives Jeffie his bottle and puts him down for a nap. "Joanie," John calls as she closes Jeff's door, "bring us something to eat and come watch the lineup."

Joan hurries in with a tray of salami and cheese, hurries back for the bowl of candy, hurries in again with napkins. John motions her to his side, kisses her ear, and drapes one arm around her, his hand brushing her breasts; she is surprised by his boldness and moves away quickly. Larry luckily has noticed nothing. "Look at Bratowski," he whistles. All the football players look alike to Joan, meaty men with shy smiles who blink uneasily when their names are read. Babies, Joan thinks to herself, accepting a can of beer from John and settling down on the beanbag chair with her mending, they are nothing but big babies. She can see Larry playing football—he has a broad red face and fat shoulders—but she is always surprised to remember that John played too, in high school; John seems too lean, too frail for such rough sport, and indeed he did hurt his knee his last year, an injury that kept him out of the Army, so some good came of it. Larry, with no such injury, went straight into the Coast Guard after high school and is now, according to John, writing a novel while he works on an assembly line at an aeronautics plant nearby. Joan wonders what kind of novel a person like Larry would write. She threads her needle in the dim light and starts to sew the patch on Jeffie's corduroy rompers. Larry, turning from the television, peers at the rompers and says, "What's that you're knitting?"

"This is sewing," John tells him.

Larry nods, unwraps a chocolate football, and pops it in his mouth. "Want one?" he says, mouth full. Joan shakes her head.

"I break out," she explains.

"WHAT?"

"Nothing."

"I could have sworn I heard you say you broke out."

"No."

"Wild. Say, Joan, whatever made you decide . . ."

He stops and John, choking as if embarrassed as he opens more beer, says, "Larry wants to know what made you decide on that haircut."

"It was just an accident," she says evenly.

"The guy butchered her," John explains to Larry.

"I'll say," Larry agrees.

"It's not what she asked for. Guy just had a nervous breakdown. Right there in the shop. I told her . . ." John lies, wide-eyed, "I told her she ought to go back there and get her money."

"Waste of money," Larry says.

"But it'll grow out. Won't it, honey? It'll grow out in no time. Her hair grows really fast."

"Would it be all right if we talked about something else?" Joan asks, but she speaks just at the kickoff and the men are shouting too loudly to hear her. "You're going to wake the baby," Joan warns, but Jeffie sleeps on. Joan still wishes they'd stop shouting; there is something unsettling about it. She has never understood the rules of football and cannot follow any of the plays anyway. She is about to excuse herself and go to the bedroom and take her nail polish off when a commercial comes on, showing a chimp trying to open a bag of pretzels.

"Looks like Joanie," John says. Joan puts her beer down and stares from her husband to the TV and back again. The chimp has large, flat, shiny ears. "Did you say, 'Looks like Joanie'?" she asks. John gives her a silly smile and shrugs.

Joan stands, goes to the bedroom, closes the door, and leans against it. She sees the double bed with its ruffled plaid quilt, the overflowing ashtray on John's side, the pleated beige curtains pulled shut along the traverse rod, the clock radio gleaming, ticking in the dim afternoon light.

There is nothing here she wants or even recognizes with affection. She goes to the bureau, pulls out a scarf, ties it over her head, walks back through the door, into the living room, and out the front door.

"Where you going?" John calls. His voice is belligerent, impotent; the voice of a weak, cruel man, Joan thinks. All these years and I never knew he was weak or cruel.

She walks very fast, for she cannot permit herself to start crying around the apartments; someone might see. But she passes no one. It seems everyone in Paradise Terrace is watching TV. The sound of the football game roars at her from each closed door and she can hear it even when she stands, adjusting her scarf, in the vast sunny parking lot. She turns, eyes lowered in the glare, crying thinly, aware that the single can of beer she drank was one can too many for her. She has to go to the toilet and she has forgotten her purse. She crosses her arms over her midriff and decides to walk east, away from the freeway, toward the old orchards.

She has seen the orchards from the bedroom window but has never walked toward them before; she has imagined how pretty they will look in spring, all white and pink against the distant hills; she has imagined that by spring John will be happier with his job, and she will have made a friend or two, and Jeffie won't be sleeping so much. But it is not spring yet and Joan, hugging herself, is seriously not sure she will be here by spring. She has never thought of leaving John before. She has thought of John dying, of being killed in a car accident, or getting some disease—but she has never thought of taking Jeffie and simply leaving. She wonders how she will live. She still has her teaching certificate; she can still get a job. She will teach children on an Indian reservation perhaps, or at a camp for migrant farm workers; she will do some good with her life before she gets old and dies. She starts to cry again, loose light tears that the sunny wind blows off her face. She wishes John had never changed. She remembers how he looked the first time she saw him, so manly in his pale blue jacket, playing the piano at a garden wedding; she remembers how talented and intelligent and funny he used to be, and how she used to love him. She brushes the tears back, thinking, quickly, Of course I still do; I still do love him. *He's* the one, she thinks. *He's* the one who doesn't love me. He says I look like a monkey. He shows off for Larry; it's Larry he cares for. The tears start again.

She has to go to the toilet very badly by now, and hurries on toward the orchard. When she comes to the fence that separates it from the edge of the development project, she stops. The fence is hung with For Sale signs that clink in the wind; broken glass and cans litter the weedway, glinting. Tramps might camp here, Joan thinks. She ducks under the fence anyway, turns, and almost screams with terror as a shape bounds through the fence after her, but it is only a dog, a thin spotted hound that starts to scout around at once as if it has been here often before. Joan looks around. The trees stand short and gray in ankle-high grass; they are very old. Without their leaves, she thinks, they look even older; without their leaves and blossoms and balls of bright fruit of course they look homely. She feels an affinity with the trees standing so unadorned in the trashy grass. The dog is darting down the aisles, sniffing everything, peeing on everything, but Joan has to be more careful. She has not seen anyone all afternoon, yet there is always the possibility someone might yet see her; she chooses the tree with the thickest trunk, goes behind it, tugs her jeans down to her knees, and squats.

It feels so good. With the sun on her knotted hands and the fresh wind on her buttocks and the urine rank and yellow on the thick gray roots of the tree, Joan at last stops crying. This is how men do things, she thinks. They just do what they want when they want to do it. She reaches up and brings a twig of the tree down toward her eye. It is not quite ready to bud; it's a red pointed wrinkled thing that makes her think, unkindly, of John. She remembers how carefully he dressed this morning, how he patted shaving lotion on his cheeks until they shone, how he brushed his sweater to look nice for the game; she remembers Larry's polished loafers and pressed cotton chinos. Underneath it all, Joan thinks, releasing the twig, men are really very unattractive. She thinks of John's balls, their bruised color, their stale odor; she thinks about the flat sparse hairs on the insides of his thighs. They dress to go out, she thinks, but when they're alone with women they show their true natures. They give us the very worst of themselves. So no wonder they hate us. She is surprised and confused by this turn of her thought and wishes again she had a friend at the apartments, some woman to talk to. She pulls her pants up and rearranges her sweater. It is pleasant to have an empty bladder and to find herself no longer so angry. John has always, she reminds herself, made a joke of her ears; it is an old old joke; he means nothing by it. If she were a better sport, she would laugh it all off. He was looking forward to this game so much. It occurs to Joan that she has ruined his afternoon by just stalking off; he is probably trying to explain things to Larry right now. She picks up a stick and throws it to the dog, who ignores it. In the spring, she thinks, I will bring Jeffie here and we will have a picnic. She imagines the blanket spread out, herself in something white and ruffled, her hair grown out, Jeffie chasing a butterfly. John can come too, she thinks. She imagines John's head on her lap, his face tipped up as he smiles at her.

John and Larry are very silent when Joan lets herself back into the apartments. They are sitting up so straight in the darkened room, holding their cans of beer so primly that it takes Joan a moment to realize that both of them are quite drunk. "Worried about you," John says in a clipped, formal voice. "Thought you'd got lost."

"I'm all right," Joan says. "Are you?"

"Old Stud here threw up on the couch," Larry says. There is a nest of silver foil in his lap, paper he has peeled from the candy. "You should have seen the mess I had to clean up."

John laughs at this and Joan tries not to stare at the couch, which does not look thrown up on. "Did you really?" she asks John. John just laughs harder.

"It was these footballs, see," Larry explains, motioning toward the candy bowl. "Aren't these great footballs?"

"Best footballs I ever ate . . ." John chokes, laughing.

Larry laughs too, loudly, once, and then both are silent, staring at the TV screen.

"I went to the orchard," Joan says.

No one responds, so, as she diapers and dresses him, Joan tells Jeffie. "I went to the orchard and met a little doggie. What do doggies say?"

"Boo," says Jeffie.

"Woof woof," corrects Joan, but Jeffie's eyes are on her hair. For a second she thinks about wearing the scarf all the time, in the house and out, until her hair grows back for good, but then she thinks: No, they'll just have to get used to it. She kisses Jeffie firmly, sets him down, and sends him off to join his father. She rinses the diaper in the toilet, wrings it out, flushes the toilet, washes her hands, avoids looking at herself in the mirror, and goes out.

The men have been feeding Jeffie chocolate footballs and he already has a brown mustache around his mouth that makes him look like a miniature man himself. Disturbed, Joan warns, "No more," but the words are scarcely out of her mouth before Larry, almost absentmindedly, unwraps two more and hands them to Jeffie. "I said, 'No more.'"

Joan stands, picks up the candy dish, and sets it on the top bookshelf by their wedding picture.

"Be a sport," Larry says. "Joan's a bad sport," he says to John.

"Do you want Jeff to get sick?" Joan asks John.

John looks from one to the other of them without saying a word. He is unnaturally white. Joan has not seen him this drunk in years; she is afraid he is going to slip to the floor and pass out and leave her alone with Larry. "I'd better make coffee," she says. She is measuring the scoops into the percolator when she hears both men leap to their feet and start shouting. "Two more minutes," John yells into the kitchen. Joan smiles at this because that means the game will be over soon and Larry can go home. But the two minutes stretch on and on and it is not until she has finished washing the plates and has poured the hot coffee into cups that she hears the men shout again.

"Did we win?" she asks, carrying the coffee out, but John and Larry have brought the candy dish down from the shelf and are pelting each other with chocolates and laughing too hard to answer. Joan sets the tray down and scoops Jeffie up in her arms; he has a piece of candy in each clenched fist and screams when she tries to take it away. She sets him down in his playpen where the men can't stampede him and goes into the bathroom to adjust her jeans; there is something in the back pocket, a small rock, a bead, something caught inside her underpants—a leaf from the apple tree?—that is pinching her, hard. As she pulls down her jeans her fingers brush something as pointed and woody as the tip of the tree twig; she looks down and sees a huge black bug—it must be a tick—burrowed headfirst into one of her buttocks. She screams and then, before either John or Larry can reach her, she rushes to lock the bathroom door. "What's the matter?" John says, outside the door. "Wan' me to break the damn door down, darlin'?"

"No!" She tries to speak with some control. "I have a tick. I mean, there's a wood tick or something in my side. A big black . . ."

She looks down. The tick seems as big as a bullet and the soft white flesh on her bottom has swollen like pink clouds around it.

"Better be careful." Larry's voice sounds behind John. "Ticks go straight for the heart."

"They do?" Joan looks down, gasping; the tick is indeed on her left side.

"Yeah. They don't stop until they get to the heart. Even if it takes them a week. They just keep plowing on. I heard about this one poor fellow . . . well . . . I'm not going to scare you. You know how to get it out?"

"No! How?"

"Best thing to do," Larry slurs, "is to burn it."

"Burn it?"

"How'd you get a tick?" John asks. "God. She goes out by herself for five goddamned minutes and she gets a goddamned tick. How'd you get a goddamned tick, honey?"

"Burning's the best," Larry says. "You got a match?"

"No!"

"Open the door, honey," John says. "I'll use my lighter."

"You both stay away from me," Joan screams. "I've had it with you both."

"She's had it with us both," Larry says.

"You have to leave her alone when she's like this," John says. "Can't do a thing with her she gets like this." He and Larry laugh softly, weakly, outside the door. Joan, alive and lucid with hatred, remembers a girl at camp telling her, years ago, that ticks are shaped like little corkscrews, and can be unscrewed, backwards. Her face set, she reaches down and grips the kicking black body; she twists until she hears something snap. Good, she thinks; it can't reach my heart now. She throws the black part that broke off into the toilet, pats some of John's shaving lotion over the puncture, washes her hands, blows her nose, and pulls up her pants. I will go to the doctor tomorrow, she thinks, and have a tetanus shot. Then I will drive with Jeffie to the airport.

She opens the door. John is standing alone in the hallway. He looks rumpled and ill. "Guess I've said some stupid things today."

"Yes. Has Larry gone home?"

"Not yet. He's trying to convince me I ought to go out with him tonight and celebrate. You know. The game."

"Celebrate the game? Of course, John. You ought to go and celebrate the game."

"It's okay with you?"

"I want you to go."

"Don't scream, Joan. If you want me to stay home, I will. Look, get me the tweezers. I'll take that tick out for you."

"You're not coming near me."

"All right. Jesus, I said I was sorry."

Joan, wheeling around, fists clenched, ready to tell him he has said nothing of the sort, ready to scream, really scream, sees such genuine bewilderment on his face that she stops. "What are you so upset about?" he asks. He asks as if he wants to know. And she sees herself, as she sometimes does see herself, through his eyes: she sees a hysterical woman upset by little things—by a haircut, an old joke, a piece of chocolate, an insect bite. To John, these mean nothing. He tries to put his arms around her, tries to tilt her wild eyes up to his. "I don't understand," he says, "why you get so upset. Don't you know that I love you?"

In a minute, maybe less, she is going to say, "No, I don't. I don't feel that you love me." She is going to say this and John is going to trap her in his thin familiar arms and she is going to turn away from his breath, which has been made

sour and rich by chocolate and beer and cigarettes, and he is
going to tell her he loves her more than he has loved anything
in the world, always has and always will; he is going to tell
her he adores her, that if it weren't for her and Jeffie he
would have nothing, be no one; he is going to bring her closer
to him as he speaks; he is going to tip her chin and stare into
her eyes and Joan will stare away; she will not look back. She
will resist. For a minute. Maybe less. And then she'll give in.
She'll give in, she'll give up, she'll give out, she'll give, and
John will draw the gift of her in with his words and his face,
the frail length of his body. She will start to flow into him as
she has always flowed and she will see him drown, dazzled,
in her free flowing, and she will see Larry, beyond John, stop
in the hallway and look lost for a moment, but not even
Larry's loud, "Ah ha. I've caught them. They're having an
orgy," will make her smile or feel any triumph; nothing anyone can ever do or say will change the regret she feels in this
ignoble flowing or wipe away the two new lines that have
already formed at each side of her mouth.

The Planter Box

Sometimes he felt she just wasn't trying. She kept the curtains drawn and the windows shut; sunlight gave her a headache and fresh air made her cough. He offered to carry her out. He had always been strong. He could carry her out to the pool and set her down in the shade; he'd carry her right into the water, if she'd let him—would she let him? The water was warm today, the wind had died down . . . No? Okay, a drive then, the doctors all said she could go for a drive. They could drive up the coast. They could drive to the wine country. He'd do whatever she wanted. What did she want?

He stood in the dark by her bed in his bathing trunks, a glass of bourbon in his hand. His voice was loud in the quiet room. Would she join him for cocktails? She shook her head. Nothing to drink? All right. How about soup? He'd bought a new kind of soup. No soup? All right. "You're a tough customer," he told her. He'd eat the soup. He ate everything he cooked anyway, everything the neighbors brought; he was hungry all day. She never touched the trays he brought in; they sat by her feet until he came to remove them. There were two trays there now; the room was a mess. She would not let him vacuum; she would not let him dust. He broke things, she said. He made too much noise. When he tried to change the sheets she'd cursed him so he'd blinked and backed down. Most of the mess she'd made herself. She pushed all the glossy new novels over to his side of the bed; sometimes he'd wake up at three, four in the morning and find their sharp corners jabbing his chest. Newspapers she simply shoved to the floor. She'd thrown a bathrobe over the television and a bed jacket over the clock radio; she didn't like the way the clock glowed in the dark, she said; she didn't need to know that much about the time. He found himself telling her the time all the same. "Getting close to five . . ." he began. She closed her eyes. The doorbell rang. "Now who could that be?" He made his voice deliberately expectant and lifted his eyebrows. He'd asked the Matthewses to drop by after work and they'd promised to try. The Matthewses had just come back from China and they'd also just bought a new computer; it would do her good to talk to people who were going places and trying new things. It would cheer her up.

He set his drink down, hitched up the waistband of his bathing trunks, and padded in his rubber thongs toward the front door. The Matthewses weren't outside; no one was outside. He had to blink against the light and readjust his glasses before he saw the big foil-wrapped pot of blue chrysanthemums left sitting by the side of the door. She wouldn't like them. She used to like flowers—she used to be quite a gardener—but now all she said was "What's the point?"

He picked the pot up anyway and carried it into the bedroom. "Surprise," he said. She frowned and held her hand out for the card. He gave it to her and carried the flowers out to the back with the others. The utility room was beginning to look like a florist shop. He put the pot on top of the washing machine and bent to smell the flowers before he left—they smelled good to him, sharp and clean and spicy—like her, he thought, they smell like her.

"Who sent those chrysanthemums?" he asked when he returned.

"No one."

"No one sent those blue chrysanthemums?"

"We didn't get any blue chrysanthemums."

"I carried them in. I saw . . ."

"There's no such thing," she said, "as a blue chrysanthemum."

It was hard for her to talk, he knew; the cancer had spread to both lungs and her throat was raw from the coughing, but her voice, although weak, was still deep as a man's. It had always tickled him to hear such a deep voice come from such a small woman. "You don't know the difference between a tulip and a calla lily," she said.

"So I made a mistake once."

"You've made a lot of mistakes," she coughed, "a lot more than once."

He finished his drink, watching her. It seemed to him there was more color in her face today. Propped up against the pillows, her hair in one long braid, her eyes huge and dark, she looked like a child, a ten-year-old girl. Her freckles stood out. He smiled. "Know something?" he said. "You're still the best looking broad in town."

"Oh sure," she said. She pushed the card that had come with the flowers toward him with the side of her finger; he picked it up and sat down on the chair by the bed, his thighs thudding against the rattan.

"Clark and Alice," he said, reading the card. "Hey! Isn't that nice?" He turned the little card over in his hands. "We'll have to call and thank them."

"They could try calling us instead," she said. "No one ever calls us. I suppose you told everyone I'm too weak to talk." She reached for her cigarettes.

"I don't tell anyone anything," he said. He stared at the card in his hand. "So Clark and Alice sent the chrysanthemums."

"No one sent chrysanthemums," she said, exhaling.

"Whatever," he sighed. He placed the card on the night table and scanned the litter—the Kleenex, the ashtray, the hand cream, the photo of the dog, the three diamond rings she wore when guests came, the glass of ice water, untouched, the glass of milk, untouched. "Time for your pill?"

She shrugged. "Who keeps track?"

"I do. I'm your nurse." He waited for her to smile; she did not.

"Some nurse. When was the last time you remembered to give me a pill?"

"Last night."

"Last night you were passed out on the couch at seven o'clock."

"So now there's a law against taking a nap?"

"There's no law," she said. "About anything." She lay back, the cigarette loose in her fingers. He wished she would at least let him cut her nails. She had started to let them grow in the hospital and now they were so long they were beginning to curl under at the tips. They reminded him of an Edgar Allan Poe story he had read as a boy, a gruesomely illustrated story about a woman who had been buried alive. She saw him looking at her hands and her slight half-smile made him look away quickly. His voice rose, belligerent. "I told you to be careful taking those pills," he said. "You're not careful, you'll really get sick."

"The pills don't do any good," she said. "Nothing does any good."

She fell asleep. He took the burning cigarette from her hand and stubbed it out. That's all we need, he thought. The house will burn down and kill us both. He stared at her. So thin. Her face in sleep so still. He patted the covers near her hand, sighed, and stood up.

It was five in the afternoon and he had nothing to do. He made himself another drink and stood in the living room. Bright yellow sunlight fell through the windows, gilding the dust on the table tops and drowning the colors of the television. He kept the television on all day now; this was the fifth or sixth time today he'd watched the news. The news, he thought again, should be called the olds. He went into the kitchen, opened the refrigerator, ate some chocolate cookies from a package, pried one crusted noodle off the top of a casserole, and chewed it slowly as he stared down at the sink of soiled dishes. Then he stood at the screen door, looking out. After a while he realized he was playing with the door, bouncing it open and shut with one finger. This was not how he'd planned to spend his first year of retirement; this was not, to tell the truth, the life he'd wish on a dog, but then he didn't want to start comparing himself to a dog because most dogs he knew had it better than most people he knew. Look at Fat Albert. The bedspread still stank of beagle, even after two years, and there was steak in the freezer with his name still on it. She used to feed him at the table and sing to him in French. He laughed, remembering, and shook his head. "Nut," he said, softly. He was not a superstitious man but it seemed to him that everything started to go wrong right after Fat Albert died, and that dog had died there by the pool, he'd snapped at a bee and the bee had somehow stung him in the windpipe—how could these things happen?—and she'd started to scream, prying Albert's mouth open, yelling "Do something! Do something!" and he'd tried but he didn't know what to do and Albert was dead by the time he brought the car around, and after that things went downhill. They'd had that one good trip to Spain together and they'd seen their daughter in Portland, and then this. Without warning: this.

He bounced the door wide, wider, widest, and went outside, careful to catch it before it slammed; he did not want to wake her. Outside, the sunlight made him feel dizzy. A tiny white butterfly danced over the leaf-littered swimming pool and darted into one of the big redwood planter boxes

where she had started a garden last year. The weeds were
blonde as straw, but when he parted them and peered in he
was amazed to see how much was growing. There were
small green tomato plants with tiny yellow flowers, and
young dill, and parsley; her vegetable garden had reseeded
itself. He lifted his head and smiled up toward the sky. The
white butterfly spiraled like a happy thought above his
head. He put his drink down and began to pull at the
weeds; they came up easily, in long sheaves like wheat, with
clods of good rich dirt in their roots. He banged the dirt
back into the planter and pulled up another handful. He
could still get this place in shape. He could get a real garden
going: corn, pole beans, beefsteak tomatoes. He'd line the
borders of the box with marigolds, to keep the snails out,
and he'd write to a seed place or find some fancy nursery
and get flats and flats of chrysanthemums, sky blue chrysanthemums—hundreds of them—that would make her sit
up and take notice. She always thought she knew everything. He'd get the pool filter fixed and maybe hire a real
nurse to oversee her medication; he might get her a dog,
another puppy, puppies always made her smile. Once she
started to smile again she'd start to eat again and then her
strength would come back and pretty soon she'd be her old
self and they might still make it to Greece by October; mir-
acles happened, new cures were being invented every day,
people got better, look at him, he'd hurt his knee in football,
broken his shoulder twice, he'd always recovered, and she
would too.

He straightened, his back stiff, and looked up toward the
oak trees for the butterfly, but it was growing dark and
nothing moved. Calla lilies still bloomed over Fat Albert's
grave; he'd have to tell her that; he'd have to tell her that the
lilies bloomed longer than tulips. He wiped his face and
finished his drink. When he looked down again he saw he'd
made a mess in the planter; it had been impossible to pull

out the weeds without uprooting the dill and parsley too; most of the little tomato plants were bent or broken; all were peppered with dirt. The whole box suddenly reminded him of the illustration from the Edgar Allan Poe story, and he saw that woman's hand clawing through, bent and hideous in its fight for life, terrible, and yet—that woman was fighting. She ought to fight too. Fight? He could see her frown at him as she drew in on her cigarette. Fight for what? Fight against what? You have never, she'd told him, faced one second of reality. Never one second in your whole life. She had said that to him on the way home from the hospital. You're coming home to get better, he'd said. I'm coming home because they can't do anything for me, she'd corrected. Because they can't even operate. And he had started to cry and she had stared at him with hatred, with rage and hatred. I'm coming home to die, she'd said, and the sooner the better.

Pie Dance

I don't know what to do about my husband's new wife. She won't come in. She sits on the front porch and smokes. She won't knock or ring the bell, and the only way I know she's there at all is because the dog points in the living room. The minute I see Stray standing with one paw up and his tail straight out I say, "Shhh. It's Pauline." I stroke his coarse fur and lean on the broom and we wait. We hear the creak of a board, the click of a purse, a cigarette being lit, a sad, tiny cough. At last I give up and open the door. "Pauline?" The afternoon light hurts my eyes. "Would you like to come in?"

"No," says Pauline.

Sometimes she sits on the stoop, picking at the paint, and sometimes she sits on the edge of an empty planter box. Today she's perched on the railing. She frowns when she sees me and lifts her small chin. She wears the same black velvet jacket she always wears, the same formal silk blouse, the same huge dark glasses. "Just passing by," she explains.

I nod. Pauline lives thirty miles to the east, in the city, with Konrad. "Passing by" would take her one toll bridge, one freeway, and two backcountry roads from their flat. But lies are the least of our problems, Pauline's and mine, so I nod again, bunch my bathrobe a little tighter around my waist, try to cover one bare foot with the other, and repeat my invitation. She shakes her head so vigorously the railing lurches. "Konrad," she says in her high young voice, "expects me. You know how he is."

I do, or I did—I'm not sure I know now—but I nod, and she flushes, staring so hard at something right behind me that I turn too and tell Stray, who is still posing in the doorway, to cancel the act and come say hello. Stray drops his front paw and pads forward, nose to the ground. Pauline blows cigarette smoke into the wisteria vine and draws her feet close to the railing. "What kind is it?" she asks, looking down.

I tell her we don't know, we think he's part Irish setter and part golden retriever; what happened was someone drove him out here to the country and abandoned him and he howled outside our house until one of the children let him come in. Pauline nods as if this were very interesting and says, "Oh really?" but I stop abruptly; I know I am boring. I am growing dull as Mrs. Dixon, Konrad's mother, who goes on and on about her poodle and who, for a time, actually sent us birthday cards and Christmas presents signed with a poodle paw print. I clasp the broom with both hands and gaze fondly at Stray. I am too young to love a dog; at the same time I am beginning to realize there isn't that much to love in this world. So when Pauline says, "Can it do tricks?" I try to keep the rush of passion from my eyes; I try to keep my voice down.

"He can dance," I admit.

"How great," she says, swaying on the railing. "Truly great."

"Yes," I agree. I do not elaborate. I do not tell Pauline that at night, when the children are asleep, I often dance with him. Nor do I confess that the two of us, Stray and I, have outgrown the waltz and are deep into reggae. Stray is a gay and affable partner, willing to learn, delighted to lead. I could boast about him forever, but Pauline, I see, already looks tired. "And you?" I ask. "How have you been?"

For answer she coughs, flexing her small hand so the big gold wedding ring flashes a lot in the sun; she smiles for the first time and makes a great show of pounding her heart as she coughs. She doesn't look well. She's lost weight since the marriage and seems far too pale. "Water?" I ask. "Or how about tea? We have peppermint, jasmine, mocha, and lemon."

"Oh no!" she cries, choking.

"We've honey. We've cream."

"Oh no! But thank you! So much!"

After a bit she stops coughing and resumes smoking and I realize we both are staring at Stray again. "People," Pauline says with a sigh, "are so cruel. Don't you think?"

I do; I think yes. I tell her Stray was half-starved and mangy when we found him; he had been beaten and kicked, but we gave him raw eggs and corn oil for his coat and had his ear sewn up and took him to the vet's for all the right shots and look at him now. We continue to look at him now. Stray, glad to be noticed, and flattered, immediately trots to the driveway and pees on the wheel of Pauline's new Mustang. "Of course," I complain, "he's worse than a child."

Pauline bows her head and picks one of Stray's hairs off her black velvet jacket. "I guess," she says. She smiles. She really has a very nice smile. It was the first thing I noticed when Konrad introduced us; it's a wide smile, glamorous and trembly, like a movie star's. I once dreamt I had to kiss her and it wasn't bad, I didn't mind. In the dream Konrad held us by the hair with our faces shoved together. It was claustrophobic but not at all disgusting. I remember thinking, when I awoke: Poor Konrad, he doesn't even know how to punish people, and it's a shame, because he wants to so much. Later I noticed that Pauline's lips, when she's not smiling, are exactly like Konrad's, full and loose and purplish, sad. I wonder if when they kiss they feel they're making a mirror; I would. Whether the rest of Pauline mirrors Konrad is anyone's guess. I have never seen her eyes, of course, because of the dark glasses. Her hair is blonde and so fine that the tips of her ears poke through. She is scarcely taller than one of the children, and it is difficult to think of her as Konrad's "executive assistant"; she seems a child, dressed up. She favors what the magazines call the "layered look"—I suspect because she is ashamed of her bottom. She has thin shoulders but a heavy bottom. Well, I want to tell her, who is not ashamed of their bottom. If not their bottom their thighs or their breasts or their wobbly female bellies; who among us is perfect, Pauline.

Instead of saying a word of this, of course, I sigh and say, "Some days it seems all I do is sweep up after that dog." Stray, good boy, rolls in dry leaves and vomits some grass. As if more were needed, as if Stray and I together are conducting an illustrated lecture, I swish the broom several times on the painted porch floor. The straw scrapes my toes. What Pauline doesn't know—because I haven't told her and because she won't come inside—is that I keep the broom by the front door for show. I keep it to show the Moonies, Mormons, and Jehovah's Witnesses who stop by the house that I've no time to be saved, can't be converted. I use it to lean on when I'm listening, lean on when I'm not; I use it to convince prowlers of my prowess and neighbors of my virtue; I use it for everything, in fact, but cleaning house. I feel no need to clean house, and certainly not with a broom. The rooms at my back are stacked to the rafters with dead flowers and song sheets, stuffed bears and bird nests, junk mail and seashells, but to Pauline, perhaps, my house is vast, scoured, and full of light—to Pauline, perhaps, my house is in order. But who knows, with Pauline. She gives me her beautiful smile, then drops her eyes to my bathrobe hem and gives me her faint, formal frown. She pinches the dog hair between her fingers and tries to wipe it behind a leaf on the yellowing vine.

"I don't know how you manage" is what she says. She shakes her head. "Between the dog," she says, grinding her cigarette out on the railing, "and the children . . ." She sits huddled in the wan freckled sunlight with the dead cigarette curled in the palm of her hand, and after a minute, during which neither of us can think of one more thing to say, she lights up another. "It was the children," she says at last, "I really wanted to see."

"They'll be sorry they missed you," I tell her politely.

"Yes," Pauline says. "I'd hoped . . ."

"Had you but phoned," I add, just as politely, dropping my eyes and sweeping my toes. The children are not far away. They said they were going to the end of the lane to pick blackberries for pie, but what they are actually doing is showing their bare bottoms to passing cars and screaming "Hooey hooey." I know this because little Dixie Steadman, who used to baby-sit before she got her Master's Degree in Female Processes, saw them and called me. "Why are you letting your daughters celebrate their feminity in this burlesque?" Dixie asked. Her voice was calm and reasonable and I wanted to answer, but before I could there was a brisk papery rustle and she began to read rape statistics to me, and I had to hold the phone at arm's length and finally I put it to Stray's ear and even he yawned, showing all his large yellow teeth, and then I put the receiver down, very gently, and we tiptoed away. What I'm wondering now is what "hooey" means. I'd ask Pauline, who would be only too glad to look it up for me (her curiosity and industry made her, Konrad said, an invaluable assistant, right from the start), but I'm afraid she'd mention it to Konrad and then he would start threatening to take the children away; he does that; he can't help it; it's like a nervous tic. He loves to go to court. Of course he's a lawyer, he has to. Even so, I think he overdoes it. I never understood the rush to divorce me and marry Pauline; we were fine as we were, but he says my problem is that I have no morals and perhaps he's right, perhaps I don't. Both my divorce and Pauline's wedding were executed in court, and I think both by Judge Benson. The marriage couldn't have been statelier than the dissolution, and if I were Pauline, only twenty-four and getting married for the very first time, I would have been bitter. I would have insisted on white lace or beige anyway and candles and lots of fresh flowers, but Pauline is not one to complain. Perhaps she feels lucky to be married at all; perhaps she feels lucky to be married to Konrad. Her shoulders always droop a little when she's with him, I've noticed, and she listens to him with her chin tucked in and her wrists poised, as if she were waiting to take dictation. Maybe she adores him. But if she does she must learn not to take him too seriously or treat him as if he matters; he hates that; he can't deal with that at all. I should tell her this, but there are some things she'll have to find out for herself. All I tell her is that the girls are gone, up the lane, picking berries.

"How wonderful," she says, exhaling. "Berries."

"Blackberries," I tell her. "They grow wild here. They grow all over."

"In the city," she says, making an effort, "a dinky little carton costs eighty-nine cents." She smiles. "Say you needed three cartons to make one pie," she asks me, "how much would that cost?"

I blink, one hand on my bathrobe collar.

"Two-sixty-seven." Her smile deepens, dimples. "Two-sixty-seven plus tax when you can buy a whole frozen pie for one-fifty-six, giving you a savings of one-eleven at least. They don't call them convenience foods," Pauline says, "for nothing."

"Are you sure," I ask, after a minute, "you don't want some tea?"

"Oh no!"

"Some coffee?"

"Oh no!"

"A fast glass of wine?"

She chuckles, cheerful, but will not answer. I scan the sky. It's close, but cloudless. If there were to be a thunderstorm—and we often have thunderstorms this time of year—Pauline would have to come in. Or would she? I see her, erect and dripping, defiant.

"Mrs. Dixon," I offer, "had a wonderful recipe for blackber . . ."

"Mrs. Dixon?"

For a second I almost see Pauline's eyes. They are small and tired and very angry. Then she tips her head to the sun and the glasses cloud over again.

"Konrad's mother."

"Yes," she says. She lights another cigarette, shakes the match out slowly. "I know."

"A wonderful recipe for blackberry cake. She used to say that Konrad never liked pie."

"I know."

"Just cake."

"I know."

"What I found out, Pauline, is that he likes both."

"We never eat dessert," Pauline says, her lips small and sad again. "It isn't good for us and we just don't have it."

Stray begins to bark and wheel around the garden and a second later the children appear, Letty first, her blonde hair tangled and brambly like mine, then Alicia, brown-eyed like Konrad, and then Sophie, who looks like no one un-less—yes—with her small proud head, a bit like Pauline. The children are giggling and they deliberately smash into each other as they zigzag down the driveway. "Oops," they

cry, with elaborate formality, "do forgive me. My mistake."
As they come closer we see that all three are scratched and
bloody with berry juice. One holds a Mason jar half full
and one has a leaky colander and one boasts a ruined
pocket. Pauline closes her eyes tight behind her dark glasses
and holds out her arms. The girls, giggling, jostle toward
her. They're wild for Pauline. She tells them stories about
kidnappers and lets them use her calculator. With each kiss
the wooden railing rocks and lurches; if these visits keep up
I will have to rebuild the porch, renew the insurance. I
carry the berries into the kitchen, rinse them off, and set
them to drain. When I come back outside Pauline stands
alone on the porch. Stains bloom on her blouse and along
her out-thrust chin.

"Come in," I urge, "and wash yourself off."

She shakes her head very fast and smiles at the floor.
"No," she says. "You see, I have to go."

The children are turning handsprings on the lawn, calling "Watch me! me! me!" as Stray dashes between them,
licking their faces. I walk down the driveway to see Pauline
off. As I lift my hand to wave she turns and stares past me,
toward the house; I turn too, see nothing, no one, only an
old wooden homestead, covered with yellowing vines, a cur-
tain aflutter in an upstairs window, a red door ajar on a
dark brown room.

"Thank you," she cries. Then she throws her last cigarette onto the gravel and grinds it out and gets into her car
and backs out the driveway and down to the street and
away.

Once she turns the corner I drop my hand and bite the
knuckles, hard. Then I look back at the house. Konrad
steps out, a towel gripped to his waist. He is scowling; angry, I know, because he's spent the last half hour hiding in
the shower with the cat litter box and the tortoise. He
shouts for his shoes. I find them toed out in flight, one in

the bedroom, one down the hall. As he hurries to tie them I tell him a strange thing has happened: it seems I've grown morals.

"What?" Konrad snaps. He combs his hair with his fingers when he can't find my brush.

"Us," I say. "You. Me. Pauline. It's a lot of hooey," I tell Konrad. "It is."

Konrad turns his face this way, that way, scrubs a space clear in the mirror. "Do you know what you're saying?" he says to the mirror.

I think. I think, Yes. I know what I'm saying. I'm saying good-bye. I'm saying, Go home.

And when he has gone and the girls are asleep and the house is night-still, I remember the pie. I roll out the rich dough, flute it, and fill it with berries and sugar, lemons and spice. We'll have it for breakfast, the children and I; we'll share it with Stray. "Would you like that?" I ask him. Stray thumps his tail, but he's not looking at me; his head is cocked, he's listening to something else. I listen too. A faint beat comes from the radio on the kitchen counter. Even before I turn it up I can tell it's a reggae beat, strong and sassy. I'm not sure I can catch it. Not sure I should try. Still, when Stray bows, I curtsy. And when the song starts, we dance.

What Do You Say?

My daughter and I are having lunch at the counter of Loretta's Coffee Shop. We have never been here before, but I can tell it's going to be one of our favorite places. The hamburgers are good, the decor looks as if it hasn't changed in forty years, and the clientele—mainly high school students, construction workers, and small-town merchants—doesn't seem to mind if my daughter, who is four, kicks her stool or chews with her mouth full. Right now she is humming to the Christmas carols we hear from the radio behind the counter; I have asked her to keep her voice down and as I am asking her again the glass door bangs open and Mr. Brown comes in. The people at the tables glance up at the bell and the gust of cold air, then go back to their sandwiches and their newspapers. My daughter resumes her loud happy humming. But I continue to stare.

I have not seen Mr. Brown in almost ten years, not since I divorced his son. He is very changed. He is thin now, almost gaunt, and uses a cane. His eyes are darkly shadowed in his large pale face and his coarse white hair is windblown. The minute I recognize him I know I should stand up and say hello.

Yet I don't. I say nothing. Even though he is wearing a long wool scarf I knit for him myself, I say nothing. Perhaps, I think, he will notice me. But Mr. Brown, standing six feet away, returns my stare with such a brief, unlit stare of his own—a look so remote it is almost majestic—that I realize he doesn't know who I am. He closes the door and moves toward an empty seat at the far end of the counter.

The coffee shop is decorated for Christmas. Plastic boughs hang over the windows and plastic berries bob down from the overhead lights. My daughter, still singing, spoons whipped cream off the top of her cocoa. "Don't slurp," I say. My voice is louder than it usually is when I correct her in public. If my voice is loud enough Mr. Brown may hear me. He may stop and turn and say, "Diana?" But Mr. Brown continues toward his stool and my daughter continues to slurp. She is excited about Christmas, too excited for manners. "Keep your napkin in your lap," I remind her.

"It *is* in my lap," she protests.

"No it's not. It's on the floor."

I watch Mr. Brown climb onto his stool. His left leg appears to be crippled; he has to hoist it by the knee and swing it onto the footrest. He props the cane beside him and, in a move so familiar it takes my breath away, pinches the bridge of his nose with his fingers, pushing his glasses, for a moment, to the top of his forehead. As soon as he is settled I will go to him and touch his arm. Ben, I'll say, remember me? And then I'll wait, for I know I've changed. I am not the twenty-year-old girl who crashed his Lincoln into the garage door, baited him into arguments about Vietnam, helped him stock the bird feeder on the patio. My hair is short now and beginning to gray; I've put on weight, begun to wear glasses. I'm happier now. He will see I am happier—as I, now, see he is less happy than he used to be. Still, when I say, How are you?, I will keep my smile steady and expectant, as if his answer to my question will be the old one. "Beautiful," he used to say, beaming. "I feel beautiful, Beautiful, how about you?" I will not ask about his son, my ex-husband, who is going through another divorce, nor will I ask about his wife, Billie, who died two years ago of cancer. I will not ask about the weight he has lost, or his leg. I will introduce my daughter and spell the name of my present husband, and I will say, It's just so good to see you.

"If I be good," my daughter says, "will I get everything I want? Will I get a camera? Will I get a two-wheeler?"

"I don't think you're old enough for either of those."

"If I be *good*, I said."

I take another napkin from the dispenser before us and place it in her lap. There is a snowfall of napkins at the foot of her stool, and pools of cocoa and catsup dot her place at the counter. I open my purse and check my wallet to make sure I have enough money to leave the waitress a generous tip.

The waitress is young and pretty and wears huge glittery earrings in the shape of Christmas trees that swing when she speaks. She holds the menu in front of her breasts and smiles at Mr. Brown. "I hope you're hungry today," she says. "Bud made pea soup."

"Oh?" Mr. Brown looks at the waitress as if he's never heard of pea soup. His face, framed by the twinkling red and green lights around the mirror, looks both attentive and lost. Perhaps he's gone senile. His father was senile. "Shoot me if I get like that," Mr. Brown used to say. "Drive me into the desert and ditch me." The waitress reaches up and adjusts the mistletoe pinned in her hair.

"Pea soup is your favorite."

"Oh yes." He takes the menu the waitress hands him. He is wearing the garnet ring on his right hand—class of 1936, U.C. Berkeley—and the gold wedding ring on his left. His fingernails are broad and ridged and as clean as ever. I wonder how the waitress ever got the idea that pea soup was his favorite? Clam chowder, barbecued steak, baked beans, onion rings, shrimp salad, french bread, and black walnut ice cream—those were his favorites. He used to weigh two hundred and eighty pounds and sway around his swimming pool dressed in nothing but a towel, dancing to Herb Alpert and the Tijuana Brass with a glass of Scotch in one hand and a Marlboro in the other. Would this waitress, in her earrings and mistletoe, have liked him back then? He called himself the King of the Canyon, wanted the blacks sent to Africa, thought we ought to bomb Cuba, kept a samurai sword that he had bought on a business trip to Tokyo under his bed, and tried to have the fence around his property electrified to keep the hippies out.

"All ready for Christmas?" the girl asks brightly.

Mr. Brown clears his throat. "I don't do much for Christmas," he says.

"Just going to take it easy," the girl nods. "Well, that's the best way."

How many Christmases—seven? eight?—have I spent with Mr. Brown? Dreary days. Cigarette smoke rising through the sunshine of the house in the canyon, the turkey turning on the spit in the outdoor barbecue, Billie sipping a beer, barefoot, in her bathrobe and diamonds, doing the crossword. Their son—my husband—Benjy—spent Christmas smoking dope in the bathroom and jotting notes for his thesis, which he said was going to be about tribal rites among West Coast Republicans. I sat by the windows and knit. Mr. Brown watched TV. Mr. Brown's father, on loan for the day from the rest home, batted Billie's dogs back with large knuckled hands when they tried to lick him. Just before dinner we exchanged presents. Benjy and I gave Mr. Brown peanut brittle and subscriptions to the *New Republic*. Mr. Brown gave us money. Much too much money. He's trying to own us, I warned Benjy. We can't pay you back, I explained to Mr. Brown. But Mr. Brown said he didn't want to be paid back. He said he was saving us for something big. He was saving us for his old age. He thought he'd come live with us in a room in our house, and play with our children, and work in our garden. When we tried to explain that we didn't think we'd ever have a house or a child or a garden—when we tried to explain that our generation was different from his—freer, more spontaneous—when we tried to say: Don't count on us—he waved us away. He was the only one to cry at our wedding. He hugged us both and talked about "sacrifice" and "compromise" and "fidelity," his flushed face and hot eyes so frightening that Benjy and I gripped hands and giggled.

The waitress smiles at my daughter, who ducks her head and kicks her stool. "Smile back when someone smiles at you," I tell her in a whisper.

"Not if I don't have to," my daughter whispers back.

The waitress asks if I'd like more coffee. I hesitate. I ought to go to Mr. Brown and get it over with, and then I ought to leave. But Mr. Brown's shadowed, tired, disinterested gaze, meeting mine once again in the mirror, makes me feel relaxed and expansive. If I am invisible, I reason, I can stay here all day. I can watch and listen like a ghost, a good ghost, who intends no harm. I lean my elbows on the counter and push my cup toward the girl.

"Yes please," I say. "Thank you."

Mr. Brown accepts more coffee too, and I hear the click of his spoon as he stirs in sugar. We lift our cups to our lips at the exact same instant, and at the exact same instant sip. Sipping still, I look at the clock. It is a large brown clock that says "Hudson's Hardware." It must have been here forever, and as I look at it I feel that I have been here forever too. I have a vision of the restaurant as a railway car, slipping down some track off the edge of the world, with all of us—my daughter, Mr. Brown, the waitress, the other customers—sailing off into space on a voyage that has no beginning and no end. I don't find this unpleasant, and I am sorry when an aproned boy comes out of the kitchen, picks the radio off the shelf, and carries it out with him, taking the Christmas music away.

"Bud made pea soup." The waitress's voice, insistent, floats down the counter.

"I'm not very hungry today," Mr. Brown says. "I think I'll just have some toast. Maybe an egg."

"And how would you like your egg?"

Mr. Brown doesn't answer.

"The usual?" the girl persists.

"That would be fine," he says mildly.

"We can't stay here all day." I rouse myself and turn to my daughter. "We've got a lot to do. Are you almost through?"

"If I be good . . ." my daughter begins.

"Yes," I prompt.

"Will I get everything I want? All the time? Always?"

"No one gets everything they want." This is an old speech, one I've given again and again. My daughter listens, chewing, her thoughts on her camera. Good is usually rewarded, I assure her. Mischief usually is not. Most people get what they deserve. I wipe her chin, wondering how this applies to Mr. Brown. What did he do to deserve to end up here, in Loretta's Coffee Shop, old and ill and so alone? He was never a tolerant man. He repeated the same jokes over and over. He ate and drank and smoked to excess. But he used to stand with his arms around the garbage bags, staring up at the moon, and he used to take his glasses off and wipe his eyes when he laughed. He never cheated or lied and he never personally ordered napalm poured on babies, as Benjy claimed. Benjy detested him. But I never did. I liked the way he confronted things: head on. When he and Benjy argued it was like watching a dog fight a cat: he would lunge straight for the heart of the question, while Benjy, evasive, leapt from side to side, answering each question with another of his own. These fights usually happened during television commercials. Mr. Brown would switch the sound off with his remote control, lean back in his leather recliner, and ask Benjy to explain to him once again why he was studying anthropology in college instead of business education: did he expect it to help him in the real world? "What do you call the real world?" Benjy would ask. "I call the real world the real world," Mr. Brown would shout, "damnit!" Benjy would grin as if he had just scored a point, but I never understood the point. Benjy and I could have used some definitions of "real world"; we weren't convinced it existed. Mr. Brown was. He still is. He is facing the mirror unadorned and unsmiling. When he looks up at the clock he sees the time and does not try to escape the time with visions of railway cars sailing through space.

My daughter reminds me of her presence by spilling her cocoa all over the counter; I sop it up with handfuls of thin paper napkins. "It was a accident," she explains in her unhushed voice. "Everybody has accidents." The waitress brings a cloth and helps me clean up as Mr. Brown, unnoticing, raises a piece of toast and bites down. His dentures make the same old click. Benjy would snort at the sound of that click, snort helplessly, unhappily, trying to catch my eye. Sometimes I'd grin back at him; sometimes I wouldn't. It was so easy to see how Benjy, with his notebook and his giggle, drove his father crazy, and I saw too how Mr. Brown, massive and complacent, made Benjy want to smash him. I stayed out of it. But by the time I left—by the time Benjy and I agreed that "sacrifice" and "compromise" and "fidelity" were real words in a real world we hadn't yet entered—by the time the marriage ended, I had contempt for them both. Shall I go to Mr. Brown and tell him that? Shall I take all the old angers and shake them over his breakfast plate? It doesn't matter if you don't remember me, I will say. You never did know me well. You used to call me Beautiful because you couldn't always remember my name. I wasn't important to you. Benjy was important to you, but you didn't think Benjy was an important person. In the end, I didn't either. In the end I disliked your boy as much as you did; I found him young and lacking too. You won, I'll say to Mr. Brown.

Mr. Brown reaches in the breast pocket of his shirt and pulls out a packet of cigarettes—not Marlboros but something lighter, with less nicotine and tar. The waitress, earrings dangling, strikes a match for him. For a second, leaning forward, with both hands clasped around his lit cigarette, Mr. Brown looks like the King of the Canyon again, regal and at ease. Then he coughs. The cough takes me as much by surprise as it seems to take him. The force of it lurches him sideways. He might lose his balance and fall off the stool, and I slip from my own stool, ready to catch him. I see myself breaking his fall, cradling his head; I imagine myself pushing the stiff white unwashed hair back from the staring eyes. It's all right, I will say. I'm here. I've come back. Diana is here, ready to take care of you in your old age.

But Mr. Brown composes himself and does not fall. The long quivering afterwaves of his cough fade as I pay my bill, leave my tip. The waitress reaches over the cash register and hands a small cellophane-wrapped candy cane to my daughter.

"What do you say?" I ask as my daughter takes it.

She will not answer.

"What do you say?" I repeat.

"I have to go to the bathroom," she says at last.

"The bathroom?"

"There's a rest room down there." The waitress points past Mr. Brown and I see we have to pass directly behind him. As we near him, I pause. The scarf I knit is close enough to touch, and it is stained and unraveled. I could offer to fix it. I still have the yarn. It wasn't that long ago, the summer I knit it. I remember sitting under the oak trees, listening to the splash from the swimming pool as Mr. Brown dove in, the clink of ice cubes from Billie's gin-and-tonic, the thud of a basketball as Benjy threw it again and again against the side of the house. My head was empty that summer except for the ticktock of knit-and-purl, and as I shook the scarf out over my bare sunburned legs I thought how nice it would look when it was finished, and how pleased Mr. Brown would be to have something from me. My daughter pulls at one hand and even as I follow her I am imagining how my other hand will look on Mr. Brown's shoulder, how I will pivot him gently, and gently say, Hello.

Peril

J oan kneels on the dirt in her old blue jeans, a package
of carrot seeds clutched to her heart. No one can see
her, which is good, because if they could see her they
would decide she was crazy. She may be crazy. She
may need to see Dr. Lippman tomorrow. The tremor and
flush she is feeling out here, alone in her garden on a Sunday afternoon, may be the first signs of a nervous breakdown. No one should fear putting seeds in the ground.
Seeds are just seeds. Joan opens her eyes, stares at the illustration on the packet: five slim golden carrots, like a
spread of sunburned fingers. Then she studies the minus-
cule, beige-colored specks in her palm, and bows her head
again. Please, she prays. Please. Her mind blanks. She never knows what to pray for. Please let them live, she thinks.
Don't let me kill them.

She draws a furrow through the raked earth with her
trowel, then another and another. Frowning, she begins to
sprinkle the seeds. They crowd and drift, as she knew they
would, already lost, as she knew they'd be. The drawstring
on her sweat shirt dangles before her as she works, and
sweat greases her forehead and chin. She can hear traffic
behind the hedge that separates the yard from the street.
Now and then her son's motorcycle coughs into life from
inside the garage; the telephone rings in the distance for her
daughter. When the back door bangs open she can hear

John, at the piano; it must be half-time in the football game he's been watching all day. John is playing something new; he starts and stops, then starts again. Joan empties the packet, waiting for him to find the melody. Then she pats the earth flat, leans back, and sighs. A car screeches to a halt in the street. A man screams, "Watch out!" and an orange kitten leaps the hedge to land beside her.

"Keep your goddamn cat inside your goddamn yard," the man yells.

"It's not my cat," Joan yells back.

But the man guns his motor and takes off down the hill.

The kitten crouches by Joan's knees. She puts a hand over it, feeling for broken bones. The kitten starts to purr. She tips its chin back to see its face. Small amber eyes meet hers with a rush of ready trust; the purr thickens. Maybe it belongs to the people across the street, she thinks. She does not know the people across the street. She and John have lived on Lansdale Avenue for almost five years, but know very few neighbors. She stands, the cat tucked under her chin, walks to the gate, checks the street for traffic, and crosses. The man across the street is unloading firewood from the back of a pickup truck.

"Excuse me," Joan says, walking up to him, "but I think I've found your kitten." She tries to disengage the little cat, but its claws have dug in and caught in her sweat shirt.

"I don't know who that cat belongs to," the man says, not looking up. "It's been following me around all day."

"Oh," Joan says. She stands by the man as he continues working. She looks up and down the street. Lansdale Avenue bisects the village. At the foot of the street there is a small shopping center with a liquor store, a bicycle shop, and a laundromat; then comes a block or two of bungalows and summer houses, then the street rises to the Cape Cod style houses of Squirrel Ridge, where she and John live.

Above Squirrel Ridge are the huge new redwood and glass houses of Lansdale Heights at the top of the hill. "I guess I should go from door to door," Joan says. The man doesn't answer. She strokes the cat and walks back across the street.

"You're not going to like this," she says as she walks into the living room.

John looks up from the piano bench. He has the television on but the sound turned off, and the football players seem to be crashing into each other in time to his chord changes. He stops playing and frowns. "Don't feed it," he says.

Joan walks past John and goes down the hall. Her daughter Jillian is sitting on the floor of the hall, talking on the telephone. "Guess what I found," Joan says. She kneels and places the cat on Jillian's lap. Jillian lifts an eyebrow—a sophisticated gesture, Joan thinks, for an eleven-year-old—and pats the cat once on the top of its head. "I can't believe he said that," she says into the telephone.

Joan picks the cat up again and takes it into the kitchen. Her son Jeffery is leaning against the sink drinking milk from a milk carton and eating peanut butter out of the jar with his finger.

"Did you wash your hands?" Joan says severely. "That grease you use on your motorcycle is extremely poisonous."

"Aaagh," gags Jeffery, clutching his stomach and reeling back.

"It is," Joan insists. "You know it too." She sets the cat on the kitchen floor and smiles as it starts to sniff at Jeffery's boots. "What do you think?"

"Looks a lot like a cat."

"It is."

"Looks a lot like an ordinary cat. I thought you said our next cat was going to be something fancy, Mom, like a Persian."

This is true. Joan has been going into pet stores lately. "Just looking," she sings out, when the salespeople come to help her. She looks at everything—the bright fish in their dark glass tanks, the tropical birds, the mice—but she has been particularly drawn to a large gray Persian kitten that has been kept caged in one shop in the village. The kitten has looked so hot and cross and bedraggled, and Joan has hated to see it dozing in its own soiled litter box. She has thought about buying that kitten, just to save it. "Persians," she tells Jeffery now, "are two hundred dollars apiece. And this isn't our 'next cat.' It belongs to someone. You can tell."

"Sure you can," Jeffery says. He grins, bends down, and offers a finger capped with peanut butter. The kitten comes and licks with quick, dainty, ravenous flicks.

"Don't let it lick any motor oil," Joan warns.

"God, Mom. You worry too much." Jeffery shakes his head, wipes his hands on his jeans, and turns to go back into the garage. As he opens the back door the dog and the other three cats come bounding inside. Joan is ready to swoop down and rescue the kitten, but she sees there is no need. The kitten crouches and hisses and the other four animals freeze in shock. Then the old cats spit, their ears flat, and the dog starts to bark. "No Brandy, no Fluffy, no Polly, no MacHeath," Joan chants. The kitten growls staunchly below her. "This is Peanut Butter," Joan says, introducing the kitten. "Peanut Butter is going to stay with us a while." She gives the dog a piece of cheese and puts him outside. She gives Fluffy, Polly, and MacHeath a plate of dry kibble, pushing it close to their flat hissing faces. She carries the kitten to another corner of the kitchen and puts him before a saucer of milk. "We are not going to fight," she announces. "We are going to behave like ladies and gentlemen." The cats eat, their eyes on each other. While the kitten is drinking its milk, Joan lifts its tail and sees what she expected: two small beige balls, neat as acorns. A male. When he is through with the milk she gives him cold meat loaf, breaking it into bits with her fingers. Then she puts him outside on the sun deck. "You'll be safe here," she tells him. She checks on him several times during the evening. Once she sees him playing with a leaf, bouncing across the deck like a blown leaf himself. Just before she goes to bed she slips another saucer of milk out the door. When John says, "Where'd you put that damn cat?" she says, in all honesty, "Don't worry. It's out."

But Jeffery lets it in early the next morning and at six Joan hears John yell, "That does it," from the kitchen. She rolls over to John's side and hugs his cool pillow. John starts to stomp and curse from the kitchen. He seems to get angrier and angrier every day. When she asks him what's wrong, he says, Nothing. I'm happy. I love you, he says. That's what he tells her. Joan wonders what he tells Dr. Lippman. She closes her eyes and pretends to be asleep when John stomps back into the bedroom. He sets her coffee cup down so hard she can hear it spill on the nightstand. "Get rid of that thing today," he says. "I mean it. Your other cats are bad enough. I hate cats," he says. "I have always hated cats. If you don't get rid of it today I'm taking it to the pound tonight."

"I work today," Joan reminds him. She is a teacher's aide at Jillian's school and she is scheduled for yard duty and library hours. "I'll put some ads around," she promises.

John interrupts her. "I'm tired of living in a zoo," he shouts. His face is very pale and there are shadows under his eyes. Joan sits up and sips her coffee. She is becoming angry herself and she hopes John will leave soon. But he stops in the doorway. "It's my new song," he says. "I'm stuck on the bridge."

"Your song?" Joan lets out her breath and puts down

her cup. John is always bad-tempered until he gets his songs just right.

"Come in and listen," he says. "Maybe you'll know what I'm doing wrong."

He walks toward the living room and Joan quickly disentangles herself from the bedclothes and follows. She curls in the armchair beside the piano, her bare feet tucked under her long flannel gown. She will listen as carefully as she can. It has been a long time since John has asked for her opinion.

"It's called 'Blues for Vivaldi,'" John says. He laughs. Joan starts to laugh too but the first chords astonish her so much she is left with her mouth open. They are dissonant, loose, almost ugly chords, and the melody John picks out is shrill and as monotonous as wings beating or crickets scraping inside a cage. She listens to the song and hears anger, panic, a great fight to get free. She stares at John. He looks the same. His mouth has the slack expression it always gets when he concentrates, his tie is loosened, his hair, just beginning to gray, falls over his forehead in familiar waves. "This is the part I can't get," John says, and plays some notes over. "I don't have the end right yet either," he adds.

"It's the best thing you've ever composed," Joan says when he's finished.

"You always say that."

"It's the most powerful thing you've ever composed," Joan amends. "There's something about it . . ."

"The bridge," John nods. He retightens his tie, picks up his briefcase, and stands. Joan trails him to the front door, reluctant to let him leave.

"That song," she says. "What's it about?"

"Oh," John says. "You know. Time running out."

"Time running out?"

"Like now," John says. He taps his watch, kisses her

good-bye, and leaves. Jeffery follows him out the door, fastening the strap of his motorcycle helmet.

"Drive carefully, both of you," Joan calls out. She goes into the kitchen, opens the jar of vitamin pills, and sets the jar in front of Jillian, who is reading her horoscope and picking raisins out of her toast. Then she goes to the back door and peers out for the kitten. He is asleep on a deck chair. She pulls some cards from her recipe box and turns them to the back, so the "Here's What's Cookin'" on the front can't be seen. In big letters she prints: "Found. Male Tiger Kitten. Very Cute." She puts her phone number and address on the card and underlines "Very Cute." She stops on her way to Jillian's school to post one card to a new redwood fence on Lansdale Heights; she tacks another to a telephone pole on Squirrel Ridge, and the third she leaves on the laundromat bulletin board. Jillian waits inside the car, applying lip gloss with her little finger, eyebrows raised as she looks in the mirror.

At the lunch recess Joan walks around the schoolyard, stooping to tie shoelaces, help with stuck thermos caps. Her job is to make sure the lower-level children pick up their lunch rubbish, play safely, and share the sports equipment; she is also supposed to break up fistfights and keep an eye out for older teenagers who might be trying to sell marijuana or pills. So far she has not had to do this, but she is glad nonetheless when Cliff Iverson, who is six feet three, walks up and joins her. "You've been getting some sun," Cliff announces, staring closely down into her face.

"Gardening," Joan admits. She smiles. She likes Cliff Iverson. His wife, Sandy, has cancer, and Cliff has had to nurse her. Cliff teaches Social Studies, and lends her books and records he thinks she might enjoy. "I'm putting in a winter garden this year," Joan says. "Carrots. And things."

"You garden too?" Cliff says. His voice is loud and

amazed and Joan looks at him quickly, wondering if he is making fun of her. She can't always tell with Cliff. He shakes back his hair, which is long and gray and not too clean. "You're quite some woman, Joan Bartlett. You make your own bread. You bake the best apple pies. You've got the little hoodlums here eating out of your hand. You're kind to strangers. You take in stray animals."

"We have a new one now," Joan says. She laughs as Cliff slaps his forehead. She can see his eyes peering out at her from under his fingers. He seems to be staring at her bosom. She half turns aside and calls, needlessly, "Be careful," as two fourth-grade girls skip past. "A little stray tiger cat," she says. "John says I can't keep it."

"Does John tell you what to do?" Cliff asks. He is still staring at her bosom.

"No," Joan says. "Of course not."

"Do you tell him what to do?"

"No." She smiles, confused. "Neither one of us tells the other," she says.

"Obviously you don't talk at all then," Cliff says.

Joan can think of nothing to say to this, but somehow she doesn't have to, for one of the skipping girls drops to her knees and screams. Joan hurries to help her, aware of Cliff's eyes still on her, on her hips this time. She finds herself bending more gracefully than she might otherwise as she helps the girl up and examines the wound, which is shallow but bloody and which will require prompt washing to avoid infection.

The kitten is waiting for her that afternoon at the back door. Joan says his name—Peanut Butter—and picks him up. She kisses the top of his head, his chin, the soft seam where his ears join his neck, his neck itself. His fur smells like outdoors and his purr is loud with health. She wishes he could stay a kitten, young and strong, forever. She thinks of Sandy Iverson, Cliff's wife, who just last summer won the women's singles at the tennis club. Now Sandy weighs less than a hundred pounds and has to wear a wig. These things happen so suddenly. No one can prepare for them. She remembers Cliff's eyes on her, frowns, and sets the cat down. Oh what does he want? she thinks irritably. Why does he look so unkempt and malnourished? She thinks of Cliff sitting by Sandy's bed, feeding her soup, wiping her chin; that is the picture of him she wishes to keep.

She is glad when John comes home. He comes home late on Mondays after his appointment with Dr. Lippman. He pours himself a beer and turns on the football game. "I'm so hungry," he says, "I could eat a cat." Joan brings him two meat-loaf sandwiches on homemade bread and stays to take a sip from the beer he offers as he watches the game. He puts his arm around her, pats her hip, and lets her go. Jillian, who has been picking all the bits of onion and green pepper out of her sandwich, looks up and smiles slightly. Jeffery, stretched out on the floor, smiles too. Joan reminds them to chew slowly and not yell at touchdowns with their mouths full. Then she goes to the back door and puts out more milk and tuna for the kitten.

When everyone has been fed, she takes her book and sits at the polished dining room table, all alone. The book is one Cliff Iverson lent her. Cliff called it a "cult book," an underground classic. Joan finds it pornographic. Several times she puts it down but then she picks it up again. She makes herself read on. It is important, she tells herself, to learn new things. She is still reading when she goes to bed that night, and she wakes up at three in the morning with a headache. It seems to her that John is awake too, he lies so still beside her. She moves close and presses against his back, but it is impossible to tell; he does not make a sound. Somewhere down in the village a siren sounds and Joan presses closer, glad that her own children are safe in their beds. "Don't," John says, or she thinks he says; the word is so indistinct he might have said nothing. But she thinks he said, "Don't." She withdraws her arm and rolls on her back on her side of the bed. "I wish Jeffery would sell that motorcycle," she says out loud. She falls back asleep and does not wake up until John drops the kitten on the end of the bed.

"It was sleeping on my car," he says. His voice is aggrieved but not really angry. "There are little paw prints all over the hood."

"Oh dear," Joan says. The cat nuzzles her armpit.

"You can keep it," John says, "if you'll let me take Fluffy and MacHeath to the pound instead; Fluffy threw up on the kitchen floor and MacHeath got into the garbage again." He kisses her, a nice, strong, coffee-flavored, married-morning kiss. Everything's all right, Joan thinks. "I've got to go," John says again.

Joan feeds the animals, picks the garbage off the kitchen floor, washes the kitchen floor, gets dressed, goes to the cleaners. At the supermarket she buys cream and liver and flea powder; she hesitates at the produce section (are her pies really "the best"?) and buys a bag of green apples. She does not stop to look in the pet store. As she lets herself into the front door she hears the phone ring. An angry woman's voice says, "Do you still have that cat?"

"Why yes," Joan says, setting down the groceries. "It's here."

"I came by this morning but you were out," the woman snaps. There is a long pause. "So I guess I'll have to get in the car and drive down again. Right?"

"Down?"

"You stuck your card right on my fence," the woman says. "The new redwood fence I built especially to keep that cat from running off. The one that cost almost a thousand dollars. That one."

"Oh," Joan says. She remembers the fence on Lansdale Heights. "Well. I'll have him ready for you."

The woman hangs up. Joan goes around the house, calling the kitten. He's asleep in the laundry basket. She picks him up and carries him into the front yard to wait. The sun feels good on her back as she walks back and forth and the purr of the cat against her chest feels warm and good too. "I'll miss you," she says. "But you come from a good home, and it's time to go back. I've enjoyed our time together. I'm glad I got to know you." She can't think of anything more to say; she feels as awkward talking to the kitten as she sometimes does talking to John or the children. She starts to hum but stops when she realizes the tune—sad and shrill—comes from John's last song. She walks back and forth in silence and is almost relieved when she hears a car door slam.

The woman fumbling with the gate is about Joan's age, but she is prettier than Joan; she has stylishly frizzed hair and wears a lavender silk shirt. A small blonde boy in a private school uniform is with her. "There's your Tom-Tom," the woman says to the boy. Joan holds the kitten out with a smile; the boy grabs it and begins to ruffle its stomach. "He can climb right over that fence," the woman says to Joan. "So what am I supposed to do? Stay home every weekend? My son already spends every weekend with his father in the city. That leaves me and the cat." Joan nods. Her eyes are drawn to the woman's shoes. They are lavender jogging shoes. They look like silk too. "I'll have to lock him in when I leave," the woman says. "But then he'll stink up the house." She twists a hand through the gold chains hung at her neck. "Happy?" she says to her son. They turn to go.

Joan tries to catch the kitten's eyes to say good-bye but he is poised and purring on the boy's shoulder. "He's a wonderful little cat," Joan says. The boy looks past her and the woman waves in dismissal. It is not until they have driven off that Joan realizes neither one of them said thank you to her. I fed that cat for two days, she thinks. I saved its life. Without me that cat would have gone to the pound or been killed by dogs or been run over. I gave it food and milk and shelter for two whole days.

It is absurd to feel hurt by someone else's rudeness. Joan tells herself this. It does not work. She feels hurt. She hugs her arms and says, "You're welcome," in a bitter voice, then laughs. Anyone watching would think she was crazy. She feels a little crazy. She has crazy thoughts. She thinks that John is going to leave her, Cliff Iverson is going to seduce her, Jillian is going to reject her, and Jeffery is going to replace her, and she thinks all these things are going to happen soon, before she is ready, if anyone can be ready, ever, for disaster. Because disaster, Joan thinks, as she walks to the hose and turns it on, is always out there, waiting to fall down on somebody's head. She drags the hose toward the carrot bed. Either John or Jeffery has taken the nozzle off for one of their own projects, and she has to spray the water on the carrots through her bent thumb. The distribution is uneven. Water sprinkles on her good brown shoes and runs down her arm. Some of the seeds are going to be drowned by this, she thinks. Some are going to bloat and pop. Others will be washed away, and others yet will be left to die, high and dry. It's a miracle, she thinks, that anything survives at all in this world. She looks all around her. No one can see. She bows her head. She prays.

Self-Defense

I t is May today, warm and so summery that I ruin
every form letter I type. By noon there is a golden
gleam to the dark office walls, and by late afternoon
the city air smells distinctly like roses. I open all the windows and lean out to breathe. "Wasting time again," David
says, shaking his head, and I have to admit that I am, that
I do, that time and I are at odds. Surely yesterday was
October? And the day before, June? "Just so long as
you're not planning to jump," David says. "I'd have nothing pretty to look at in here if you jumped." I turn from the
window, astonished, and David scowls at me and blushes.

David is my boss; he is also my friend; he is twenty-seven
and I am thirty-eight, so friendship was indicated right
from the start; he listens, sad-faced, to my jokes, and I
listen, yawning, to his advice; we agree completely on the
essential uselessness of McVeigh, Stone, and Farland; we
eat lunch together in the park on fine days and play chess in
the Employee's Lounge when it rains; we loan each other
scratched Frank Sinatra records and talk about things we'd
do if we didn't have to work. We have what David calls a
"fellowship" rather than a relationship, and so this compli-
ment (pretty to look at?) confuses me. I ignore it. I tell
David that I would never throw myself out of a window. A
moron might, I say. Morons are big on windows. David

shakes his head. "Not another of your moron jokes," he begs.

"No one likes them," I admit. "Even Amanda, with her bad taste . . ." My voice trails away. Amanda, my seventeen-year-old daughter, has advised me not to smile too much when I talk. "Your face wrinkles more than it used to," she's explained, "and you look sort of old and tired, like somebody's mother."

"Amanda's right," David says. He places his smooth hand next to mine on the windowsill, "I mean, why date yourself when you could date someone else?" He grins. His own jokes are even feebler than mine. "*Gone with the Wind* is playing downtown. That's about your speed. Want to go see it? With me? Sometime?"

I shrug and say, sure. Sometime would be fine. But in the meantime: I ask David if he knows why the moron threw a cube of butter out the window. No? So he could see a butterfly! Does he know why the moron threw a clock out the window? No again? To see if time itself could fly . . .

"Tonight?" David says. "What are you doing tonight, for instance."

Tonight I have to drive Amanda someplace. For a moment I'm so flustered I can't remember what place, and then I do—tonight's her night for Self-Defense. I'm very sorry, I tell David. I turn my palm up on the windowsill so he won't notice how red and wrinkled my knuckles are. My hand is shaking a little.

"Can't she drive herself?" David asks.

The thought of Amanda driving makes me shudder. Oh no, I say. Amanda? No.

"She's old enough, isn't she?" David persists.

Amanda's old enough, I agree. It's just that . . . well, Amanda's a poet, of sorts, and not very practical; she's usually lost in some book or some dream and I just wouldn't trust her behind the wheel of a car, not yet.

"So you're still tied down," David says, and he says it with such finality that all the way home I think about this and wonder if he's right. It's been two years now since Amanda's father left to marry one of his students, and while I no longer cry myself to sleep at night I have not yet begun to feel the giddy freedom that being single is supposed to bring women these days either. Partly it's my job, which is just that, a job, and not a "career," and partly it's because I do—David's right—feel responsible for Amanda. But look at Amanda. Who wouldn't feel responsible?

Here she is, my seventeen-year-old daughter, lying on the front porch of our house in her black bikini as I come home from work; her hands are crossed over her heart, there are dead and dying flowers in her hair, her toenails are painted three shades of purple. When she sees me coming she flattens along the porch and says, "What's the password? No, don't even stop to think about it. And don't look at me either. I'll tell you. The password today is 'fat.'"

"You look like Ophelia," I say, stepping over her with my arms full of groceries.

"Was Ophelia fat?"

"She had other problems, Amanda."

Amanda groans and rolls over. "I wish," she says. That's all she says. I look down at her and then I look past her into the garden. I am delighted to see that my old yellow roses have once again burst into gala festoons against the unpainted fence. I should have gone out with David, I think. What harm could it do? We would have had a fine, friendly time.

"What a beautiful time of year this is," I say, holding the groceries in my arms like a dance partner.

"It just makes me lonely," Amanda replies. "It just makes me want to die." She reaches for the book propped under her head, opens it, and begins to read. It is a book of poems about suicide; the woman who wrote it smiles cleverly over a cigarette from the dust jacket; she is dead now. "I love this part," Amanda says, and reads a line out loud, but I am thinking instead of Amanda's poem, the one she showed me after her father's last phone call. "How will Death come? Like salt on my tongue," Amanda's poem read.

"You're getting awfully morbid," I start to say, but the phone is ringing and it might be for me, it might be David saying he's lied about his age from the start. But the voice is Lena's, bright and too cheerful.

"Don't tell me," Lena says, "that Amanda actually is letting someone else talk on the telephone for once. What's the matter? Is she off her feed?"

"She seems preoccupied with death today," I say. I pour a glass of Chablis and stand by the phone and listen to Lena, who, like me, lives alone with a teenager, and whose teenager is changing, as mine is changing, into someone new, unknown, and not entirely likeable.

"He acts more like his father every day," she says for the third time and then, abruptly, "Let's go out, Jill. *Gone with the Wind* is playing downtown; let's go see it. It will cheer us up, remind us of what it was like when men were men and women weren't. Don't you want some romance in your life?"

I do, I admit it. But I can't go out. I have to take Amanda to Self-Defense.

"What on earth does Amanda need Self-Defense for?" Lena wonders. "You and I are the ones who need care and protection."

"What *do* you need a Self-Defense class for?" I ask Amanda at dinner.

"Credit," Amanda says. She reaches for the salt and shakes it over everything on her plate. "I flunked Driver's Ed, remember, and then I had to take an Incomplete in Foods, and then they cancelled my Human Diseases and

Insect Psychology classes so this is the only class I can take. It's worth five school credits. I need it to graduate."

"What happened to World History?" I ask. "What happened to Geometry? Literature? Latin? Physics?"

"Get with it, lady," Amanda says. She snaps her fingers and smiles. The phone rings again, and again it's not David. Amanda talks in the pressured, giggling, explosive vocabulary she uses with her friends. She plays with the saltshaker as she talks, shaking salt onto the table and drawing stars and exclamation points in it. I take the salt away at last and hide it in the cupboard; I sponge the table, do the dishes, sweep the floor. Fool, I hear Lena saying in my head. We're the ones who need care and protection.

I decide to take a bath before driving Amanda back to the high school. I close the bathroom door, run the cool water. I lean back in the tub, slowly soaping, looking at the broken veins in my legs, the silver zigzag stretch marks down my belly, the rosy bumps on my nipples. Where did my body collect all these scars? Some of them are as old as Amanda, but others, bruises, callouses, are defects I have failed to see before. I wonder what David would think of this body. Something pretty to look at? I don't think so. No. I don't. Not even David could say something so courtly, and yet, I think, turning one ankle back and forth in the air, the legs aren't so bad, the breasts haven't fallen, perhaps in the dark . . .

"Mom?" Amanda says, outside the door. "I have to be there in half an hour. If you don't want to drive me, though, I can probably find a ride."

"With whom?"

"I don't know. Someone."

"Are you talking about hitchhiking, Amanda?"

Amanda doesn't answer. I narrow my eyes and sink up to my chin in the water. "Because if you are . . ." I threaten. I have still not recovered from the shock of seeing her standing by the freeway; she was wearing her flowered hat and my high heels and she was walking backwards with her thumb stuck out. At first I didn't recognize her; I just thought: there's a dumb girl looking for trouble. She recognized me, of course, at once, and the minute I braked she tried to run. I had to drag her inside the car, my nails deep in her arm. I remember how our voices rose, high and frightened, tangled in accusation and protest by the side of the roadway.

"Mom?" she says again. "Are you going to drive me or not?"

"You know I am."

"I know," Amanda agrees.

My chin sinks lower into the cool unclean water as Amanda, humming, moves down the hallway to change in her room.

It is still light and still warm and the air still smells like roses when we leave. Amanda throws herself over the back of the car seat to unroll the windows. The old station wagon shakes as she churns at the handles. She is wearing too much makeup and too little clothing, but I don't notice this until I've pulled out of the driveway. "Don't tell me," she says, folding her arms. "You think I look fat."

"It's not fat," I say, glancing again at the torn shorts, the short black sweater worn without a bra, the strand of pink plastic pearls, the frizzed hair with the yellow rose stuck in it, the mascara, the lip gloss. "It's not fat," I repeat, "it's . . ."

But Amanda strikes her bare knee with her fist before I can form the old-fashioned word "cheap."

"Look at that," she says, of her knee, which is round and brown and simple. "Doesn't that make you sick? It makes *me* sick, I hate my whole body," she says. "Sometimes I wish I was a cloud. Then I could float away. Or a mountain. I look fat as a mountain."

I drive in silence, thinking of Amanda, in pink pearls, becoming a mountain. I see her volcanic on the front porch, in her bikini, blocking the door. "I am a pimple oozing purple pus," one of her poems read. "I am a sty in a dead pig's eye."

Amanda strikes her knee again. "I can't wait until next year," she says.

"What happens next year?"

"I'll be eighteen. I'll be free. I can do what I want. I think I'll just take off and travel."

"Travel where?"

"You know," Amanda says. "Around."

"And how will you support yourself?"

"I can always find a job," she says, her voice trailing away. "I can wait tables. Or be a cowgirl. Maybe I could be a field worker. I've always wanted to be a field worker."

"Amanda . . ."

"I'm not going to college, that's all I know. So let's not talk about it now. I hate it when you want to talk about things. I wish . . ." Amanda says. She smooths down her shorts, leans over, and kisses me quickly as I let her out in front of the high school. "The class will be over in two hours," she says. For a second she looks worried. "Don't forget me."

I watch her walk across the grass. She walks as she has walked since she was ten months old, with her hands fanned out as if she were balancing on a high wire, and her back straight, and her beautiful knees slightly stiff. Other women are also walking across the grass. Some are my age, some are even younger than Amanda, little girls in pigtails. They all look expectant, as if the class they are going to is fun. I wonder what I shall do, this warm May night, for fun. I certainly do not feel like wrestling a bunch of other women in a classroom for credit. That is not my idea of fun. Nor, I realize, is going home to an empty house. There isn't time for a movie and there's too much time to just sit in a cafe nursing a coffee. I decide to call Lena and see if she wants to meet me; we could sit in a bar somewhere and talk. I want to talk, I want to tell someone about David. I want to explain that what happened caught me by surprise; in my surprise I thought he felt more than "fellowship" for me and so of course I had to act stern and maternal, to discourage him. And now, I will tell Lena, I feel like a fool.

The first phone booth I find is outside a corner grocery store; it smells of spilled soda pop and beer. Teenage boys in swimsuits gather outside the store as I dial Lena's number; their voices are unhappy and teasing, their bodies are perfect. Lena is not home and as I hang up and step back onto the street I realize I am completely invisible to the boys on the sidewalk. I wonder if they would see me if I were Amanda's age, and I smile because I know they would, and this seems odd, for I truly feel no different now than I did at seventeen. At seventeen I was just as absentminded, just as unambitious, just as overwhelmed by the odor of roses. I said "I wish" all the time, like Amanda does, and I wrote poems too—but such conventional poems, about gypsies and moonlight and storms at sea. I never wrote about pus in a pig's eye. It never occurred to me to hate my knees. I would have been terrified to hitchhike, and I would never have shown my poems to my mother, as Amanda, almost aggressively, shows them to me.

I get in the car, start the engine, and drive halfway down the broad bare block before I realize, again, that I have nowhere to go, nothing to do. What will it be like next year, if Amanda does leave home? What will it be like when I'm

not "still tied down"? Will I be caught up in some mad
social whirl of being wined and dined by twenty-seven-year-
olds? Oh I doubt it, I do indeed doubt it. Maybe, though,
I'll finally quit my job and take the time to think about
finding work I enjoy. Maybe I'll go back to school and
finish my degree. I might even follow Amanda's lead and
sell the house and travel. Travel? Amanda? I see my dazed,
lazy, garlanded daughter as a waitress in Denver, a motel
maid in Dallas. She has never worked. She flunks courses in
school. She can't even drive.

"Don't worry about me," Amanda says.

"Worry about yourself," Lena advises.

Well, I do. Alone in my car, going nowhere slowly down
a street in broad daylight, I do worry about myself. Yesterday I was seventeen; tomorrow, at this rate, I'll be seventy.
Time is going by too fast, and it doesn't seem to be taking
me with it. I pass the park Amanda played in as a baby;
other children play there now while other mothers watch. I
reach for the radio and snap it on. The station I like plays
old songs, but at the sound of Frank Sinatra crooning "Angel Eyes" I snap it off again. David's eyes change color in
the light; they changed from green to hazel to yellow when
he said, "Tonight? What are you doing tonight, for instance?" It was that yellow that stopped me; I'm cautious,
I slow. Old lines from my own adolescence come into my
mind: I'm afraid of becoming involved. I don't want to
get hurt. What if David touches me? I think. What will I
do? Will I know how to touch back? Lena said all she could
do was lie there and cry when she took her first lover; he
never called back and after a week of waiting she drove to
the beach. "The boy was with his father," she told me, "so
I lay in the sun all day and when it was time to go home I
couldn't go home. I sat on the sand and watched the sun
set and then I sat on, unable to move. I stayed there all

night. I was afraid if I got up I'd walk straight into the ocean and disappear. I was afraid no one would miss me if I did disappear."

Driving away from the ocean I end up at the library. I park and go in. I will read something light for pleasure on this warm golden night. I choose two novels, but I can't concentrate on either. At last I settle in the reading room and flip through magazines. I mean to read an article in the *National Geographic;* I mean to study *Time.* Instead I find myself staring at page after page of a fashion magazine. I read an article about cancer of the cervix and another about plastic surgery and another about the poet Amanda likes, who killed herself when her husband left her. I feel I have read these articles before, often before. When I look up it's dark outside, and when I stand I see my own reflection in the reading room windows. With my ruffled hair and shadowed eyes I look like somebody's mother.

Amanda's classroom is brightly lit and from the cries and cheers coming from the open door it's apparent the class isn't over yet. As I cross the grass and come to the door I see Amanda in the center of the room, with the women circled around her. She is holding her hands out like a tight-rope dancer and her knees are stiff. A man comes up behind her. "Our cop," the little girl in pigtails whispers to me. "He helps teach the course. His name is Teddy, and he's a real bear," she grins.

"Hello, baby," the policeman says, and lunges for my daughter. Amanda screams and I scream too. The little girl laughs. "Watch this," the little girl says. The man grabs Amanda around the neck and starts to twist her backwards toward the floor. Amanda's mouth opens wide, terrified, her teeth flash, her arms swing helplessly. Rose petals scatter from her hair. As she twists to spin free her pearls break and bounce over the floor, and her sweater lifts briefly over chubby bare breasts. In another second she is free, running, with an angry, satisfied look on her face that doesn't change even when she turns and whacks her hip against a desk. The policeman wipes his face, grins, and says, "Good girl. You made it this time. Next?"

A blonde woman about my age steps forward. As Teddy the Bear twists her arm and forces her easily toward the floor, I look around the room. It is an ordinary classroom, with a sink and rows of low tables. A poster on the bulletin board says, "The Devil Made Me Do It." A myna bird in a cage by the window emits a low, worldly whistle as the women scream, "Kick him! Scratch him! Bite!" Amanda moves happily over the floor on her hands and knees, picking up pearls. The little girl helps her.

"And now," the policeman is saying, "here's what to do if someone tries to force you into their car. Say you're walking along the roadway and someone tries to grab you. You ought to know how to break their hold."

Amanda, crouching on the floor, looks up to watch the policeman. I watch Amanda.

"Next week," Amanda says as we cross the grass toward the parking lot, "we're getting a new cop to work with. We need experience with different physiques. This new cop is supposed to be tall and faster than Teddy." She sighs, content. "And what did you do?" she asks me. I tell her I went to the library and read magazines. "Old mom," Amanda says. She pats my waist. "Good old mom."

The way she says this makes me so angry I stop. Amanda, humming, stops beside me. I am aware of her height, her weight, her physical strength as we stand in the dark. She is grown up, I think. She is almost as tall as her father.

"I'm glad I told you about my plans," Amanda continues dreamily. "It's going to be so great when I go. I've decided I'm going to move to the desert and write poetry there; at first I thought the beach, but then I thought, Nope, I don't want anyone seeing me in a bathing suit. In the desert you can wear a caftan and no one has to know how fat you are."

"In the defense class you can wear a bra," I snap. "So no one has to know how naked you are."

"Mom!" Amanda says, shocked.

"I think you dress like a tramp," I say, throwing caution to the wind. "And I'd like to know how you think you're going to get to the desert or anyplace else without me to drive you."

"What's the matter with you?" Amanda says. "Getting there is the least of my worries."

"Oddly enough," I tell her, "it's the very first of mine." I hand her the car keys.

"What are those for?"

"We're going to have a driving lesson. Here, in the parking lot."

"I don't want to take a driving lesson now, Mom. I flunked Driver's Ed. Remember? Besides, it's dark."

"Get in."

"No. Come off it. Please. It's late. I'm hot. I'm really tired, Mother."

"I'm tired too." I hear my voice rise, shrill in the darkness, and I hear the truth of the words inside the shrillness—the truth I've been fighting off with moron jokes and form letters and little favors for Amanda. I'm tired, and I'm depressed, and I'm lonely, and I'm mad, and I'm scared to death of almost everything in the world—and I don't want to stay like this too much longer. I want to bloom, soon; I want to touch and be touched. I turn my back on Amanda, open the car door, and sit down hard in the passenger's seat; it seems strange to sit here again after all these years; it makes me feel vulnerable, it makes me feel small. I cross my arms and wait. At last Amanda, silent, slips in beside me and grips the wheel.

"Okay," she says. "Since you want to die."

"I don't want to die," I assure her. The scent of sweat and roses fills the car as I show her where the headlights are, and how to release the brake, and how to change the radio to a rock-and-roll station. She grinds the key in the ignition and we start off with a lurch.

"This is going to take a long, long time," Amanda warns. Arms crossed, tired to the bone, I tell her that's fine; time means nothing to me.

Rough Translations

There was so much to do that Ramona felt dizzy, and when Ramona felt dizzy, Ramona lay down; once down she stayed for the count and then some. Shadow and sun took their turns on her ceiling, the phone rang unanswered, a Mozart sonata spun silently on the turntable by the window. Ramona dozed, and dreamed she was dancing. When she awoke she found her own hands clinging to her own ribs as if for dear life. It's the funeral, she decided. It's the funeral that's killing me.

She must have spoken out loud because her son Potter stared from the doorway. He was balancing a bag of groceries in one arm and his pet cat and violin case in the other. In his slipped-down glasses and long brown ponytail he looked as careworn as any young housewife, and Ramona felt the familiar urge to apologize, an urge she stifled with a shamed little laugh and a wave from the pillows. If my timing had been better, she thought, Potter could be touring Europe right now, playing music with his friends, having some fun . . . can Potter have fun? Potter frowned and said, "What is it? You okay?"

"Alive," Ramona cried gaily, "and kicking." She lifted one moccasined foot to demonstrate and knocked the phone book off the bedspread. Potter's frown deepened. He had never smiled at Ramona's jokes, nor had his sister Nora; finding their mother unamusing was the one trait they shared.

Sometimes Ramona thought: It's because they can't forgive me. Other times she thought: It's because they have no sense of humor. She watched as Potter, frowning, put down his burdens and moved into her room. He snapped the record player off, drew the curtains closed, turned the lamp on, plumped her pillows, and pressed his lips gingerly to her forehead to feel her temperature. Ramona, tucked under his chin like a violin being tuned, tried to sound the right note. "I had the funniest dream," she said, but even as she began to tell the dream she saw Potter didn't think it was funny; his face was so pained she started to lie. One lie, as always, led to another, and down she went, deeper and deeper. "So there I was," she finished, breathless, "tap-dancing among the gravestones like Ginger Rogers in a horror film. Isn't that a scream?"

"It might make a good drawing for *The Beacon*," Potter said. Ramona bowed her head, contrite. She knew what Potter thought of her drawings. She had heard him describe the cartoons she did for the village weekly as "illustrated idioms, the kind you find on cocktail napkins," which she supposed was a fair description—not kind, but fair. A few days before, propped up in bed, she had finished her last assignment: a pen and ink sketch of a little ark floating on a sea of question marks with a caption that read "Flooded by Doubts." Her very favorite submission, "Tour de Force," had showed a docent dragging a group of tourists through the Louvre at gunpoint, and it was true she had seen a cartoon much like it etched onto a highball glass at the church rummage sale; she had bought the glass, of course, and pitched it into a garbage bin at once. She tried now to imagine how she would draw her dancing dream. She'd sketch herself as she was: a small, wide-eyed old woman with bad posture and a frizz of gray bangs. She'd dress herself in a straw hat and tux and set herself among the headstones at Valley View . . . Valley View? Was that right? Was that the cemetery she had finally decided on? Or was that the one where Hale had been buried? Should she be buried by Hale after all? Would he want her there? Would he let her stay? Her fingers started to clutch at her ribs again, and again she sighed and said, "So much to do. So many decisions. I hope you never have to go through this, Potter."

"Right," said Potter. He replaced the phone book on the bed, gave Ramona another of his shy hard stares, and left with the cat meowing at his heels to start cooking their dinner.

Ramona reached for her glasses, picked up the phone book, and turned again to the back. She had memorized the five listings for Funerals, but she had not yet found the nerve to dial. She stared at the ads again, narrowing in on the Manis Funeral Home, which said, "Call at Any Time," and The Evergreens, which advertised air-conditioned chapels. The air-conditioning tempted her, for the summer afternoons had been growing warm, but when she finally started to dial and her finger slipped, she took it as an omen. She did not think the Manis Home, despite its insistence, should receive calls at dinner time; she'd call them tomorrow too.

She fell into her old habit of reading the phone book, leafing through the classifieds for Mourners, then for Paid Professional Mourners, then finally for Mummers. She still wondered where Hale had found that little blonde who wept so competently at his graveside—a waitress Ramona had not been told about? an extra secretary? How delicious it would be, she thought, if I could hire the equivalent of that little blonde—some good-looking young boy, an acting student down on his luck . . . someone who would be willing to fling himself down on the coffin . . . She shivered happily, thinking how that would shock Nora, and then, penitent, she reached for the phone again and dialed Nora's number, the words "I hate to bother you" already forming on her lips. She knew Nora would be busy. Nora was always busy. Right now, Ramona feared, Nora would be kneading a loaf of whole wheat bran bread, knitting a sweater, cutting the baby's hair, balancing her husband's business accounts, checking the twins' homework, and drafting a proposal for a new gymnasium while her old mother, with nothing better to do, lay slumped in a filthy bathrobe on an unmade bed covered with overdue library books, wanting a chat. Oh Lord, Ramona thought, gazing around her cluttered room, but Potter and I live like two French whores, underwear everywhere, and jars full of dead roses. I can never have the funeral here. The best thing to do is go to Nora's at once and get buried in Nora's backyard like a pet hamster in a shoe box.

"I can't decide between the Manis or The Evergreens," she said, when Nora picked up the phone. "How can I find out which one is the best?"

"I'll find out for you," Nora said. "Next?"

Nora's knitting needles clicked like static on the other end of the line while Ramona tried to think of something else to ask for. "Medication?" Nora suggested. "Has Potter been giving you the right medication?"

"I think so." Ramona glanced at the bottle by the bed, rechecked it to be sure it was labeled for her and not the cat, and leaned back. "It's just planning this funeral."

"Do you know what I'd do about that funeral if I were you?" Nora said.

Ramona waited, grateful.

"I'd forget it," Nora said. "I'd file it away in my Not-to-Worry drawer."

"Not-to-Worry drawer?"

"That's right. I'd file it away and swallow the key. Do you understand?"

"I'm not a child," Ramona began, but Nora, her voice flat, sweet, and dangerous, said. "Have Potter cook you some real food for once. I'll come by and see you in the morning. I don't like the idea of you thinking about your funeral all day. It's not healthy."

Not healthy? thought Ramona. That's a good one. She said good-bye to Nora and lay back. Her heart began to race and her fingers raced too, drumming and tapping on top of the phone book. What should she do, what should she do? Perhaps there was still enough time to go crazy? She had always meant to spend her last days tiptoeing around in a flowered hat with a fingertip pressed to her lips, but no luck. These were her last days and she felt no crazier than usual. She felt as she always had when there were decisions to be made: harassed and dreamy, wildly anxious and un-able to move. She reached up to twist one earring off, realiz-ing, with dismay, that one was all she was wearing; in her haste to prove she could still dress herself she had forgotten to put on the other. Her bathrobe buttons—were they closed? They were. She wished she could push a button and make herself disappear, right now, before her body became a burden to them all, before they learned how complicated, dull, and expensive it was to dispose of even a small per-son's final remains.

"You know who I admire?" she said to Potter as she joined him in the kitchen for dinner. "Junie Poole. Junie sat down in the hall outside the coroner's office one night and tried to kill herself by drinking a thermos of gin mixed with pills. When they arrested her she was too drunk to talk, but they found this note pinned to her mink coat say-ing she hoped her children would appreciate the fact that she had at least taken herself to the morgue. Of course, no one's appreciated anything Junie's ever done, before or since, but that's not the point. The point is that she did try to make things easy for her family. I want to make things easy too." She picked up her fork and looked down at her plate. "Liver? Won't Nora be impressed." She tried to eat a little. But when she saw the cat, in the corner, licking from an identical plate, she put the fork down and regarded Potter, who had done this to her before, once with canned salmon and once with pickled herring. He was either trying to be very economical or his values were more confused than she suspected. "Potter," she said, watching the old gray cat huddled murmurously over its plate, "do you think I should just crawl off to the woods?"

"There aren't any woods within crawling distance," said Potter. Ramona smiled; Potter did not. "I think . . ." Potter began. He stopped. Ramona folded her hands and waited. Potter, born when she was over forty, had been a talkative child, full of ideas and advice and so original that even Hale had paid attention, but Potter had stopped talking years ago, at least to her. "I think," Potter repeated, one thin hand fluttering before his downcast face, "that you are using this funeral to mask your real feelings."

Ramona waited, her own head bent. "And what are my real feelings?" she asked at last.

"Rage," Potter said, his shy eyes severe behind his smudged glasses. "Terror. Awe. Grief. Self-pity."

"Heavens," said Ramona. She was impressed. Once again she wished she were the mother her children deserved, and once again she found herself having to tell them she was not. "I'm afraid, Potter," she said, "you give me credit. I don't feel any more of those 'real' feelings now than I ever have. What I feel now is a sort of social panic, the same old panic I used to feel when Hale wanted me to give a dinner party for his clients and the guests would arrive and I'd still be in my slip clutching a bucket of live lobsters. I'm sorry, dear, I can't eat this. I'm too nervous. I'm going to have to make a list."

She sat at her drawing desk, staring at a piece of paper, wondering where to start after printing "To File in the Worry Drawer" across the top of the page. In the next room

Potter talked to Nora on the telephone, his voice reluctant and slow. If only my children liked each other, Ramona thought. She sighed and pressed her palm to a few of the places that hurt. Sometimes the pains were gone for hours altogether and sometimes they felt like ripping cloth; sometimes they widened and sometimes they narrowed and sometimes they overwhelmed her completely. Right now she was being treated to a new pain, a persistent jabbing in her chest that tapped back and forth like an admonishing finger. It feels like I'm being lectured by a bully, she thought. Lectured on my failures. If I had been lovable, Hale would have loved me, and if Hale had loved me, I would have loved myself, and if I'd loved myself, Nora would have loved me, and if Nora had loved me, Potter would have loved her, and then Potter wouldn't have had to grow up loving nothing but his music and his wretched cat. Hale and I, she thought, set a bad example for the children as far as loving went . . . the children! she thought. She pushed her chair back and stood up. "Tell Nora," she called out to Potter, "tell Nora I'm sorry but this is going to be an adults-only funeral, X-rated, no grandchildren allowed. Maybe the boys, but by no means the twins. By no means the baby. I've seen little children at funerals before," she added, when Potter finally returned from the phone, "and it's no picnic, believe me."

"Nora said to give you this." He handed Ramona a mug of warm milk and his eyes were so sad that she drank it all down even though there was a cat whisker floating on top.

That night Ramona dreamed her funeral was held outdoors on the slope of a mountain; it was a bright summer afternoon and everyone she'd ever cared about was there: her parents, her grandparents, Hale, all her friends from childhood on. She was there herself, hovering in the sky like a Chagall bride, her pretty shroud rippling around her crossed ankles. She had never felt so happy. Tables set up under flowering trees were laden with cakes and roasts and sparkling wines; music came from somewhere; there were rainbows, fountains. The conversations she overheard made her laugh with pleasure; people were saying kind, affectionate, funny things to each other, some of them so wonderful, so insightful, that Ramona could scarcely wait to wake up and write them down.

Half-asleep, she groped for pencil and pad and quickly, in the dark, jotted down every scrap of conversation she could remember. In the morning, unsurprised, she studied her notes. They were illegible, as frail and choppy as an EKG. Lost, she thought. Like everything else. Lost like all the words I've tried to string together throughout my life. For a brief, bitter second she thought of all the poems, stories, prayers, and revelations that had evaporated like breath in cold air when she tried to express them. I have never said anything right, she decided. Even my jokes, even the drawings I do for *The Beacon* are wrong—rough translations of a foreign language I hear but cannot master.

She took her pen and quickly tied all the choppy lines on the paper together, making a scrawl across the top, and then she drew herself at the bottom of the page, an anxious old lady staring straight up, and then she wrote "Over My Dead Body" and tore the paper up.

She shook the day's second dose of Percodan into her palm and thought again of Junie Poole passed out in front of the coroner's office. It was then she saw how her own funeral truly would be: a small gathering of silent relatives sitting in uncomfortable pews in a little Consolation Chapel somewhere. Pink and yellow light would fall through the stained-glass window over the casket where she lay. The air would smell unwholesomely floral. Muzak would be piped in. She would be wearing an evening gown that Nora, at the last minute, would have had to alter to fit, a terrible dress, mauve, with long sleeves and net at the neck. Her nails

would be painted mauve to match, and her lips. Her five
grandchildren would be wild with horror and boredom.
The boys would be thinking about basketball and sex, basketball and sex. The twins would be cracking their knuckles, glancing cross-eyed at each other, giggling. The baby,
whose damp quick hands were never still, would be digging
a design into the plush seat with a thumbnail, a design no
one but the baby would know was a skull and red flames.
Nora would be shushing and clucking the children as she
counted the heads in the chapel, trying to decide if she had
made enough potato salad. A minister chosen by Nora's
husband would give a speech. The minister would say that
Ramona was in a far better place than she had been before.
Potter, picking cat hair off his pressed blue jeans, would
think about this. He would regret he had not gone to Europe with his friends when he had the chance; he could be
in a better place, too, he would think, if it weren't for his
mother. After the ceremony the mourners would bunch on
the sidewalk in the sun, ill-at-ease and restless . . . and I'll
still be lying beneath the pink and yellow lights, Ramona
thought, reeking of hairspray and formaldehyde—and the
garnet necklace I want Nora to save for the baby will still
be around my neck, forgotten in that damn mauve net.

She eased herself out of bed, walked unsteadily toward
her closet, opened the door, and peered in. The darkness
surprised her. At first she could not see the mauve dress and
she even had a wild hope she had thrown it out, years ago,
but then she saw it, hanging in its plastic bag like a hideous
orchid. As she reached up to strike it off the clothes rod, she
lost her balance and fainted forward. It was so strange to
fall face forward into soft dark clothes that when she came
to she was not even frightened. She tried to tell Potter how
strange it had been, how comfortable, how sexy really, like
falling into outheld arms, like dancing. Oh but that time
Hale twirled her at the Christmas party and she was feeling

almost beautiful that night and so deeply in love and as she came out of the twirl Hale turned to another woman, neglecting to catch her, and she lost her balance and spun across the dance floor, all the colored lights a blur, and she was completely alone and she was laughing, even before she fell and cracked her coccyx she was laughing, prepared for the laughter of others, prepared to say, "It's all right, I'm not hurt a bit," even though it wasn't all right, even though she *was* hurt a bit. Quite a bit. Always after that she saw herself as Hale saw her: a clumsy woman with breasts that were too big and lips that were too wide and little awkward hands that couldn't hold a man. She saw herself as someone who could be dropped. "Oh Ramona bounces back," Hale drawled, and didn't she though, bouncing back like any old kickball. Well, the secret was not to take yourself too seriously. No matter where they kicked you it couldn't hurt if you didn't let it, if you got right down there with the dancing shoes and laughed—if you could do that, you could rise like a rose in the air when they toed you.

"I have something to say," she said to Potter. "I have a statement to make. Are you ready? You should write this down. It's very important. Listen, Potter. Words of wisdom: Lie low. Move fast. Bounce."

"Don't try to talk," Potter said. He knelt beside her, stroking her forehead with the same light scratchy touch he used on the cat. "Don't keep making jokes. You don't have to be funny any more. Just breathe slow. Relax."

Ramona flushed with temper and turned her head away. She could not relax. She was angry at Potter and at Hale and at Nora and at herself too, angry at everything that wasn't funny any more, angry at everyone who had let her down, down, so far down that when young Dr. Seton stood up from the chair by her bed it was as if he were stretching up toward the ceiling and she was sinking down through the floor, sinking faster and faster, and only the thought of her funeral made her stop: the last straw, she thought, and wouldn't you know it's the one straw I reach for. "Good girl," Dr. Seton said. "You're coming back to us."

Coming back? Of course she was coming back. How could she leave? There was so much to do. There was her life to understand and Hale to forgive and Nora to charm and Potter to cheer up. There was the novel. Where was the novel? Lying in a cardboard box somewhere, half-alive, unfinished, unformed. There were all the paintings, the little canvasses of pastel flower arrangements that Hale had called "stillborns" instead of "still lifes"—where were those? Facing the walls of the garage? She didn't want anyone seeing those paintings; she didn't want anyone reading the journal she had kept in the first years after Hale's death, or playing the tapes she had made of her own voice, singing her own songs to her own accompaniment on an old guitar. She was not ready to be judged; her work wasn't done yet; it wasn't begun; she didn't even know what her work was, for God's sake. "You seem to have developed a faintly comedic point of view," her last art teacher had told her. "Have you thought of doing cartoons?" And he had dismissed her, turning his head, stifling his yawn; he had dropped her, not bothering to watch the direction of his kick, nor the way it hooked, nor the way she bounced, landing on both flat, splayed, calloused feet before the editor of *The Beacon* with a sheaf of drawings in one shaking hand. She had an occupation now. But was that her work?

"Those cartoons," she said, looking up into Nora's puzzled face, "those cartoons were the hardest things I ever did and they were never what I meant to do. I meant to do something quite important and beautiful with my life, you see—something that would astonish and delight and make you all proud."

"Still trying to talk," Nora said. "Half-alive and she's still trying to talk. She's probably worried we're going to take her to the hospital. Well, don't worry, Mother. Dr. Seton said you might as well stay here—although why you'd want to, I'm sure I don't know. The house is a mess. It's filthy dirty and there's nothing in the cupboards but cat food. I've sent the boys out to rake the yard and the twins are making cocoa, and the baby, here's the baby, the baby will keep you company while I discuss a few things with Potter. And his cat."

After Nora left the room, the baby—a lanky, curt, fast-moving four-year-old whose given name, Hope, was so unsuitable that Ramona had never been able to use it—sidled close and peered down into Ramona's face. "Ba?" said Ramona. It was all she could say. "Ba? Ah wa pa."

"You. Want. Paper," the child repeated.

Ramona pointed toward her desk and Hope tugged at the drawers until she found the drawing supplies. She gave Ramona one pad and one pencil and then, engrossed, she chose a thicker pad, a sharper pencil, for herself. Ramona struggled upright in her bed. For a long time she and Hope sat quietly, thinking. Then Hope ducked over her pad and started to draw a city. Ramona sat immobile. Even if I try, she thought, I won't succeed. I've never been able to organize my life; how dare I attempt to order my death? My funeral will be as disastrous a failure as my childhood, my marriage, my motherhood, my dotage. There will be the same dry coughs, the same scraping of chairs, the same artificial smiles I've seen all my life. I'll be put to rest like all the rest, and no one will ever know how much I had to give the world, or how I longed to give it. She glanced at her granddaughter's page. Hope had finished the city and was peopling it quickly with vampires and werewolves. It's enough to make the old blood stagger, Ramona thought. In the next room Potter and Nora were arguing. The smell of burnt cocoa drifted in from the kitchen. Ramona dozed. She dreamt Hale was in bed with her, asleep, his back turned to her, his weight warm, familiar, a great comfort, and she snuggled close, glad to have him there but afraid to wake him, afraid he might awaken saying some other woman's name.

When she opened her eyes it was dark in the house. She turned on her light, picked up the pad and pencil, and began to write. She had just had the one idea that would make her funeral the successful occasion she knew it could be. She knew the music, the foods, the psalm, the location. She wrote quickly, covering the page. She wrote until she had said everything she had to say, and then, content, she slipped the paper into the top drawer of her nightstand, lay back, and slept.

It was a restless, busy, broken sleep and it seemed to go on for a long long time. Dreams came and went, some of them nightmares, some so full of light she fought to stay in them. Nora nursed her with unsmiling vigilance, bathing and dressing her with swift cool hands. Nora's children took over the house, the boys mowing and trimming the lawn, the twins scrubbing the kitchen and bathrooms. Only the baby refused to pitch in. She sat at the desk beside Ramona's bed, covering page after page with intricate, disordered drawings. Potter too ignored Nora's orders; he locked himself in his room with the cat and tuned and retuned his violin. Ramona, listening to him play over the sound of the vacuum and the dishwasher, felt a robot was playing to her from the moon, so strange and cold and simple the music. Sometimes one of the children would drag a chair to the bureau and bring her the photos she asked for—portraits of Hale, his smile lean, gleaming, and enticing as ever, group pictures of old school friends standing arm in arm in sunny gardens, photos of her own children as children and herself as child, girl, and mother. When Ramona looked from these pictures to the face in the mirror Nora held up, she was pleased. She finally had a face she liked, sharp-boned, flushed, with enormous eyes—a stylish face, at last. She still could not speak clearly enough to be understood and when visitors told her she looked beautiful she could only tip her head, a queen accepting homage. There's a price tag to all this glamour, she wanted to tell them. Nothing big. A pay-later plan.

One afternoon Nora said, "Come on, Potter, help me for once. I want to carry Mother outside." The two of them linked hands and carried Ramona out into the garden, pausing to point out the bright banks of amaryllis and filling her bathrobe skirts with Japanese plums from the un-pruned trees against the fence. Ramona looked into their pale distracted faces and said, "If you two would just like each other a little, I think I could go to heaven this second," and Nora said, "Still trying to talk? I wish she'd give up," and Potter said, "She can't give up; she's tough; she's not like us," and Nora said, "Speak for yourself; I don't slop around feeling sorry for myself all day," and Potter said, "That's because you don't know how to feel anything, period," and they carried Ramona into the house and dropped her on the bed a little too roughly. That night Potter announced that since Nora had taken over so well, he was leaving. He was moving in with another unemployed musician who had a house by the sea. "I'd like to move to a house by the sea," Ramona said suddenly, and this first clear sentence after weeks of gibberish made Potter turn and Nora stop in mid-sentence. "I'd like to go there right now," Ramona said, "and never come back."

"Don't make me cry," Nora said sharply.

"She means she wants to die," Potter said.

"I know what she means," Nora said.

Potter picked up the cat and held it close to his heart, then laid it by Ramona's side like a bouquet of gray flowers. Nora came and stood beside them. "She's asleep again," Nora said. "No I'm not," Ramona said. "There's so much

I've wanted to tell her," Nora said. "But I don't have her gift. I've never known how to put things."

"Well," Ramona answered, pleased, "I thank you and I think I finally have put things in place myself. I've taken care of everything at last." But nobody heard her. It was dark in her room and she was alone. Why look at me, she thought. I've gone and died with my big mouth wide open. She started to laugh and in that same second she started to spin, which made her laugh harder, for she knew that with this last breath she would fall, fall and break herself and bounce, bounce far beyond laughter forever.

The cat leapt off the bed and meowed for Potter, but Potter and Nora were sitting in the kitchen drinking coffee together and talking about a time when they had both thought their mother the gayest and most beautiful woman in the world, their father the richest and kindest man. The only one who heard the cat cry was the baby. The baby had slipped from her sleeping bag and was prowling through the house, searching for paper. She let herself into Ramona's room and went to the desk, but the drawers were depleted, all paper gone. In the top drawer of the nightstand by the bed she found some paper, one side ruined by her grandmother's writing, but the other side fresh and clean. She turned to the clean side and went to the window. Squatting in the moonlight with the cat winding around her, the baby drew the dream that had awakened her: a woman shooting off the edge of the planet, her lips like two red wings, flapping up toward the stars. She studied the drawing, shook her head, and tore it up.

Nora made the arrangements for the funeral. It didn't take long. She was pretty sure she knew what her mother wanted. She found a long purplish evening dress in the closet that looked brand new, and she gave it with instructions for matching nail polish to the cosmetician at The Evergreens. Her husband knew a minister who agreed to say a few words. After the service, which was mercifully short for such a warm afternoon, the mourners were asked to return to the house for refreshments. Most of the mourners seemed to be truly mourning; some of them were weeping. Ramona had been so brave, they said, so uncomplaining. She had kept her sense of humor to the end, they said, and they paused to study the display of drawings from *The Beacon*, their faces long and somber. The cat wandered companionably through the crowd. Potter sat in the garden with his violin, playing a song that everyone knew but no one could place. The notes seemed to come together in little rushes, rise, fade off, rush in again. "My Mother's Voice," Potter said, when the minister asked the name of the piece. The baby, swaying to the music, pushed open the door of Ramona's room, climbed the chair by the bureau, brought down all the photographs, and dropped them out the window, chanting "Bury Bury" as they fluttered down. She was about to throw a garnet necklace out too when her father caught her and gave her a spanking. Nora, handsome in black, was too busy to pay attention to her daughter's screams; she was telling everyone how childlike Ramona had seemed toward the end, how dependent and docile. "It was as if I were the mother . . ." Nora began, but she was interrupted by a large lady name Junie Poole who hugged her impulsively, spilling gin down her dress. "This is the best funeral I've ever been to," Junie declared, and although the others turned away to hide their smiles, they all said later they agreed. It was a good funeral. The weather was fine and sunny, the house was welcoming. The only thing missing was Ramona herself.

Previous Winners of